RECALLED TO LIFE

GRANT ALLEN

1st WORLD
LIBRARY
Literary Society

Recalled To Life

Grant Allen

© 1st World Library – Literary Society, 2004
PO Box 2211
Fairfield, IA 52556
www.1stworldlibrary.org
First Edition

LCCN: 2004195304

Softcover ISBN: 1-4218-0135-3
Hardcover ISBN: 1-4218-0035-7
eBook ISBN: 1-4218-0235-X

Purchase *"Recalled To Life"*
as a traditional bound book at:
www.1stWorldLibrary.org/purchase.asp?ISBN=1-4218-0135-3

1st World Library Literary Society is a nonprofit
organization dedicated to promoting literacy by:

- Creating a free internet library accessible from any computer worldwide.
- Hosting writing competitions and offering book publishing scholarships.

Readers interested in supporting literacy
through sponsorship, donations or
membership please contact:
literacy@1stworldlibrary.org
Check us out at: www.1stworldlibrary.ORG
and start downloading free ebooks today.

Recalled To Life
contributed by Tim, Ed & Rodney
in support of
1st World Library Literary Society

CONTENTS.

CHAPTER I.

UNA CALLINGHAM'S FIRST RECOLLECTION

It may sound odd to say so, but the very earliest fact that impressed itself on my memory was a scene that took place - so I was told - when I was eighteen years old, in my father's house, The Grange, at Woodbury.

My babyhood, my childhood, my girlhood, my school-days were all utterly blotted out by that one strange shock of horror. My past life became exactly as though it had never been. I forgot my own name. I forgot my mother-tongue. I forgot everything I had ever done or known or thought about. Except for the power to walk and stand and perform simple actions of every-day use, I became a baby in arms again, with a nurse to take care of me. The doctors told me, later, I had fallen into what they were pleased to call "a Second State." I was examined and reported upon as a Psychological Curiosity. But at the time, I knew nothing of all this. A thunderbolt, as it were, destroyed at one blow every relic, every trace of my previous existence; and I began life all over again, with that terrible scene of blood as my first birthday and practical starting point.

I remember it all even now with horrible distinctness. Each item in it photographed itself vividly on my mind's eye. I saw it as in a picture - just as clearly, just as visually. And the effect, now I look back upon it with a maturer judgment, was precisely like a photograph in another way too. It was wholly unrelated in time and space: it stood alone by itself, lighted up by a single spark, without rational connection before or after it. What led up to it all, I hadn't the very faintest idea. I only knew the Event itself took place; and I, like a statue, stood rooted in the midst of it.

And this was the Picture as, for many long months, it presented itself incessantly to my startled brain, by day and by night, awake or asleep, in colours more distinct than words can possibly paint them.

I saw myself standing in a large, square room - a very handsome old room, filled with bookshelves like a library. On one side stood a table, and on the table a box. A flash of light rendered the whole scene visible. But it wasn't light that came in through the window. It was rather like lightning, so quick it was, and clear, and short-lived, and terrible. Half-way to the door, I stood and looked in horror at the sight revealed before my eyes by that sudden flash. A man lay dead in a little pool of blood that gurgled by short jets from a wound on his left breast. I didn't even know at the moment the man was my father; though slowly, afterward, by the concurrent testimony of others, I learnt to call him so. But his relationship wasn't part of the Picture to me. There, he was only in my eyes a man - a man well past middle age, with a long white beard, now dabbled with the thick blood that kept gurgling so hatefully from the red spot in his waistcoat. He lay on his back, half-curled round toward one arm, exactly as he fell. And the revolver he had been shot with lay on the ground not far from him.

Grant Allen

But that wasn't all the Picture. The murderer was there as well as the victim. Besides the table, and the box, and the wounded man, and the pistol, I saw another figure behind, getting out of the window. It was the figure of a man, I should say about twenty-five or thirty: he had just raised himself to the ledge, and was poising to leap; for the room, as I afterwards learned, though on the ground floor, stood raised on a basement above the garden behind. I couldn't see the man's face, or any part of him, indeed, except his stooping back, and his feet, and his neck, and his elbows. But what little I saw was printed indelibly on the very fibre of my nature. I could have recognised that man anywhere if I saw him in the same attitude. I could have sworn to him in any court of justice on the strength of his back alone, so vividly did I picture it.

He was tall and thin, but he stooped like a hunchback.

There were other points worth notice in that strange mental photograph. The man was well-dressed, and had the bearing of a gentleman. Looking back upon the scene long after, when I had learned once more what words and things meant, I could feel instinctively this was no common burglar, no vulgar murderer. Whatever might have been the man's object in shooting my father, I was certain from the very first it was not mere robbery. But at the time, I'm confident, I never reasoned about his motives or his actions in any way. I merely took in the scene, as it were, passively, in a great access of horror, which rendered me incapable of sense or thought or speech or motion. I saw the table, the box, the apparatus by its side, the murdered man on the floor, the pistol lying pointed with its muzzle towards his body, the pool of blood that soaked deep into the Turkey carpet beneath, the ledge of the window, the young man's rounded back as he paused and hesitated. And I also saw, like an instantaneous flash, one hand pushed behind him, waving me off, I almost thought, with the gesture of one warning.

Why didn't I remember the murderer's face? That puzzled me long after. I must have seen him before: I must surely have been there when the crime was committed. I must have known at the moment everything about it. But the blank that came over my memory, came over it with the fatal shot. All that went before, was to me as though it were not. I recollect vaguely, as the first point in my life, that my eyes were shut hard, and darkness came over me. While they were so shut, I heard an explosion. Next moment, I believe, I opened them, and saw this Picture. No sensitive-plate could have photographed it more instantaneously, as by an electric spark, than did my retina that evening, as for months after I saw it all. In another moment, I shut my lids again, and all was over. There was darkness once more, and I was alone with my Horror.

In years then to come, I puzzled my head much as to the meaning of the Picture. Gradually, step by step, I worked some of it out, with the aid of my friends, and of the evidence tendered at the coroner's inquest. But for the moment I knew nothing of all that. I was a newborn baby again. Only with this important difference. They say our minds at birth are like a sheet of white paper, ready to take whatever impressions may fall upon them. Mine was like a sheet all covered and obscured by one hateful picture. It was weeks, I fancy, before I knew or was conscious of anything else but that. The Picture and a great Horror divided my life between them.

Recollect, I didn't even remember the murdered man was my father. I didn't recognise the room as one in our own old house at Woodbury. I didn't know anything at all except what I tell you here. I saw the corpse, the blood, the box on the table, the wires by the side, the bottles and baths and plates of an amateur photographer's kit, without knowing what they all meant. I saw even the books not as books but as visible points of colour. It had something the effect on me that it might have upon anyone else to be dropped suddenly on the stage of a theatre at the very moment when a hideous crime was being committed, and to believe it real, or rather, to know it by some vague sense as hateful and actual.

Here my history began. I date from that Picture. My second babyhood was passed in the shadow of the abiding Horror.

CHAPTER II.

BEGINNING LIFE AGAIN

What happened after is far more vague to me. Compared with the vividness of that one initial Picture, the events of the next few months have only the blurred indistinctness of all childish memories. For I was a child once more, in all save stature, and had to learn to remember things just like other children.

I will try to tell the whole tale over again exactly as it then struck me.

After the Picture, I told you, I shut my eyes in alarm for a second. When I opened them once more there was a noise, a very great noise, and my recollection is that people had burst wildly into the room, and were lifting the dead body, and bending over it in astonishment, and speaking loud to me, and staring at me. I believe they broke the door open, though that's rather inference than memory; I learnt it afterwards. Soon some of them rushed to the open window and looked out into the garden. Then, suddenly, a man gave a shout, and leaping on to the sill, jumped down in pursuit, as I thought, of the murderer. As time went on, more people flocked in; and some of them looked at the body and the pool of blood; and some of them turned round and spoke to me. But what they said or what they meant I hadn't the slightest idea. The noise of the pistol-shot still rang loud in my ears: the ineffable Horror still drowned all my senses.

After a while, another man came in, with an air of authority, and felt my pulse and my brow, and lifted me on to a sofa. But I didn't even remember there was such a thing as a doctor. I lay there for a while, quite dazed; and the man, who was kindly-looking and close-shaven and fatherly, gave me something in a glass: after which he turned round and examined the body. He looked hard at the revolver, too, and chalked its place on the ground. Then I saw no more, for two women lifted me in their arms and took me up to bed; and with that, the first scene of my childhood seemed to end entirely.

I lay in bed for a day or two, during which time I was dimly aware of much commotion going on here and there in the house; and the doctor came night and morning, and tended me carefully. I suppose I may call him the doctor now, though at the time I didn't call him so - I knew him merely as a visible figure. I don't believe I THOUGHT at all during those earliest days, or gave things names in any known language. They rather passed before me dreamily in long procession, like a vague panorama. When people spoke to me, it was like the sound of a foreign tongue. I attached no more importance to anything they said than to the cawing of the rooks in the trees by the rectory.

At the end of five days, the doctor came once more, and watched me a great deal, and spoke in a low voice with a woman in a white cap and a clean white apron who waited on me daily. As soon as he was gone, my nurse, as I learned afterwards to call her, - it's so hard not to drop into the language of everyday life when one has to describe things to other people, - my nurse got me up, with much ado and solemnity, and dressed me in a new black frock, very dismal and ugly, and put on me a black hat, with a dreary-looking veil; and took me downstairs, with the aid of a man who wore a suit of blue clothes and a queer kind of helmet. The man was of the sort I now call a policeman. These pictures are far less definite in my mind than the one that begins my second life; but still, in a vague kind of way, I pretty well remember them.

On the ground floor, nurse made me walk; and I walked out to the door, where a cab was in waiting, drawn slowly by a pair of horses. People were looking on, on either side, between the door and the cab - great crowds of people, peering eagerly forward; and two more men in blue suits were holding them off by main force from surging against me and incommoding me. I don't think they wanted to hurt me: it was rather curiosity than anger I saw in their faces. But I was afraid, and shrank back. They were eager to see me, however, and pressed forward with loud cries, so that the men in blue suits had hard work to prevent them.

I know now there were two reasons why they wanted to see me. I was the murdered man's daughter, and I was a Psychological Phenomenon.

We drove away, through green lanes, in the cab, nurse and I; and in spite of the Horror, which surrounded me always, and the Picture, which recurred every time I shut my eyes to think, I enjoyed that drive very much, with all the fresh vividness of childish pleasure. Though I learnt later I was eighteen years old at least, I was in my inner self just like a baby of ten months,

Grant Allen

going ta-ta. At the end of the drive, we drew up sharp at a house, where some more men stood about, with red bands on their caps, and took boxes from the cab and put them into a van, while nurse and I got into a different carriage, drawn quickly by a thing that went puff-puff, puff-puff. I didn't know it was a railway, and yet in a way I did. I half forgot, half remembered it. Things that I'd seen in my previous state seemed to come back to me, in fact, as soon as I saw them; or at least to be more familiar to me than things I'd never seen before. Especially afterwards. But while things were remembered, persons, I found by-and-by, were completely forgotten. Or rather, while I remembered after a while generalities, such as houses and men, recognising them in the abstract as a house, or a man, or a horse, or a baby, I forgot entirely particulars, such as the names of people and the places I had lived in. Words soon came back to me: names and facts were lost: I knew the world as a whole, not my own old part in it.

Well, not to make my story too long in these early childish stages, we went on the train, as it seemed to me, a long way across fields to Aunt Emma's. I didn't know she was Aunt Emma then for, indeed, I had never seen her before; but I remember arriving there at her pretty little cottage, and seeing a sweet old lady - barely sixty, I should say, but with smooth white hair, - who stood on the steps of the house and cried like a child, and held out her hands to me, and hugged me and kissed me. And it was there that I learned my first word. A great many times over, she spoke about "Una." She said it so often, I caught vaguely at the sound. And nurse, when she answered her, said "Una" also. Then, when Aunt Emma called me, she always said "Una." So it came to me dimly that Una meant

ME. But I didn't exactly recollect it had been my name before, though I learned in due time afterwards that I'd always been called so. However, just at first, I picked up the word as a child might pick it up; and when, some months later, I began to talk easily, I spoke of myself always in the third person as Una. I can remember with a smile now how I went one day to Aunt Emma - I, a great girl of eighteen - and held up my skirt, that I'd muddied in the street, and said to her, with great gravity:

"Una naughty girl: Una got her frock wet. Aunt Emma going to scold poor Una for being so naughty!"

Not that I often smiled, in those days; for, in spite of Aunt Emma's kindness, my second girlhood, like my first, was a very unhappy one. The Horror and the Picture pursued me too close. It was months and months before I could get rid for a moment of that persistent nightmare. And yet I had everything else on earth to make me happy. Aunt Emma lived in a pretty east-coast town, with high bracken-clad downs, and breezy common beyond; while in front stretched great sands, where I loved to race about and to play cricket and tennis. It was the loveliest town that ever you saw in your life, with a broken chancel to the grand old church, and a lighthouse on a hill, with delicious views to seaward. The doctor had sent me there (I know now) as soon as I was well enough to move, in order to get me away from the terrible associations of The Grange at Woodbury. As long as I lived in the midst of scenes which would remind me of poor father, he said, and of his tragical death, there was no hope of my recovery. The only chance for me to regain what I had lost in that moment of shock was complete change of air, of life, of surroundings. Aunt Emma, for her part, was only too glad to take me in: and as poor papa had died intestate, Aunt Emma was now, of course, my legal guardian.

She was my mother's sister, I learned as time went on; and there had been feud while he lived between her and my father. Why, I couldn't imagine. She was the sweetest old soul I ever knew, indeed, and what on earth he could have quarrelled with her about I never could fathom. She tended me so carefully that as months went by, the Horror began to decrease and my soul to become calm again. I grew gradually able to remain in a room alone for a few minutes at a time, and to sleep at night in a bed by myself, if only there was a candle, and nurse was in another bed in the same room close by me.

Yet every now and again a fresh shivering fit came on. At such times I would cover my head with the bedclothes and cower, and see the Picture even so floating visibly in mid-air like a vision before me.

My second education must have been almost as much of a business as my first had been, only rather less longsome. I had first to relearn the English language, which came back to me by degrees, much quicker, of course, than I had picked it up in my childhood. Then I had to begin again with reading, writing, and arith-metic - all new to me in a way, and all old in another. Whatever I learned and whatever I read seemed novel while I learned it, but familiar the moment I had thoroughly grasped it. To put it shortly, I could remember nothing of myself, but I could recall many things, after a time, as soon as they were told me clearly. The process was rather a process of reminding than of teaching, properly so called. But it took some years for me to recall things, even when I was reminded of them.

I spent four years at Aunt Emma's, growing gradually to my own age again. At the end of that time I was counted a girl of twenty-two, much like any other. But I was older than my age; and the shadow of the Horror pursued me incessantly.

All that time I knew, too, from what I heard said in the house that my father's murderer had never been caught, and that nobody even knew who he was, or anything definite about him. The police gave him up as an uncaught criminal. He was still at large, and might always be so. I knew this from vague hints and from vague hints alone; for whenever I tried to ask, I was hushed up at once with an air of authority.

"Una, dearest," Aunt Emma would say, in her quiet fashion, "you mustn't talk about that night. I have Dr. Wade's strict orders that nothing must be said to you about it, and above all nothing that could in any way excite or arouse you."

So I was fain to keep my peace; for though Aunt Emma was kind, she ruled me still in all things like a little girl, as I was when I came to her.

CHAPTER III.

AN UNEXPECTED VISITOR

One morning, after I'd been four whole years at Aunt Emma's, I heard a ring at the bell, and, looking over the stairs, saw a tall and handsome man in a semi-military coat, who asked in a most audible voice for Miss Callingham.

Maria, the housemaid, hesitated a moment.

"Miss Callingham's in, sir," she answered in a somewhat dubious tone; "but I don't know whether I ought to let you see her or not. My mistress is out; and I've strict orders that no strangers are to call on Miss Callingham when her aunt's not here."

And she held the door ajar in her hand undecidedly.

The tall man smiled, and seemed to me to slip a coin quietly into Maria's palm.

"So much the better," he answered, with unobtrusive persistence; "I thought Miss Moore was out. That's just why I've come. I'm an officer from Scotland Yard, and I want to see Miss Callingham - alone - most particularly."

Maria drew herself up and paused.

My heart stood still within me at this chance of enlightenment. I guessed what he meant; so I called over the stairs to her, in a tremor of excitement:

"Show the gentleman into the drawing-room, Maria. I 'll come down to him at once."

For I was dying to know the explanation of the Picture that haunted me so persistently; and as nobody at home would ever tell me anything worth knowing about it, I thought this was as good an opportunity as I could get for making a beginning towards the solution of the mystery.

Well, I ran into my own room as quick as quick could be, and set my front hair straight, and slipped on a hat and jacket (for I was in my morning dress), and then went down to the drawing-room to see the Inspector.

He rose as I entered. He was a gentleman, I felt at once. His manner was as deferential, as kind, and as considerate to my sensitiveness, as anything it's possible for you to imagine in anyone.

"I'm sorry to have to trouble you, Miss Callingham," he said, with a very gentle smile; "but I daresay you can understand yourself the object of my visit. I could have wished to come in a more authorised way; but I've been in correspondence with Miss Moore for some time past as to the desirability of reopening the inquiry with regard to your father's unfortunate death; and I thought the time might now have arrived when it would be possible to put a few questions to you personally upon that unhappy subject. Miss Moore

Grant Allen

objected to my plan. She thought it would still perhaps be prejudicial to your health - a point in which Dr. Wade, I must say, entirely agrees with her. Nevertheless, in the interests of Justice, as the murderer is still at large, I've ventured to ask you for this interview; because what I read in the newspapers about the state of your health -."

I interrupted him, astonished.

"What you read in the newspapers about the state of my health!" I repeated, thunderstruck. "Why, surely they don't put the state of MY health in the newspapers!"

For I didn't know then I was a Psychological Phenomenon.

The Inspector smiled blandly, and pulling out his pocket-book, selected a cutting from a pile that apparently all referred to me.

"You're mistaken," he said, briefly. "The newspapers, on the contrary, have treated your case at great length. See, here's the latest report. That's clipped from last Wednesday's Telegraph."

I remembered then that a paragraph of just that size had been carefully cut out of Wednesday's paper before I was allowed by Aunt Emma to read it. Aunt Emma always glanced over the paper first, indeed, and often cut out such offending paragraphs. But I never attached much importance to their absence before, because I thought it was merely a little fussy result of auntie's good old English sense of maidenly modesty. I supposed she merely meant to spare my blushes. I knew girls were often prevented on particular days from reading the papers.

But now I seized the paragraph he handed me, and read it with deep interest. It was the very first time I had seen my own name in a printed newspaper. I didn't know then how often it had figured there.

The paragraph was headed, "THE WOODBURY MURDER," and it ran something like this, as well as I can remember it:

"There are still hopes that the miscreant who shot Mr. Vivian Callingham at The Grange, at Woodbury, some four years since, may be tracked down and punished at last for his cowardly crime. It will be fresh in everyone's memory, as one of the most romantic episodes in that extraordinary tragedy, that at the precise moment of her father's death, Miss Callingham, who was present in the room during the attack, and who alone might have been a witness capable of recognising or describing the wretched assailant, lost her reason on the spot, owing to the appalling shock to her nervous system, and remained for some months in an imbecile condition. Gradually, as we have informed our readers from time to time, Miss Callingham's intellect has become stronger and stronger; and though she is still totally unable to remember spontaneously any events that occurred before her father's death, it is hoped it may be possible, by describing vividly certain trains of previous incidents, to recall them in some small degree to her imperfect memory. Dr. Thornton, of Welbeck Street, who has visited her from time to time on behalf of the Treasury, in conjunction with Dr. Wade, her own medical attendant, went down to Barton-on-the-Sea on Monday, and once more examined Miss

Callingham's intellect. Though the Doctor is judiciously reticent as to the result of his visit, it is generally believed at Barton that he thinks the young lady sufficiently recovered to undergo a regular interrogatory; and in spite of the fact that Dr. Wade is opposed to any such proceeding at present, as prejudicial to the lady's health, it is not unlikely that the Treasury may act upon their own medical official's opinion, and send down an Inspector from Scotland Yard to make inquiries direct on the subject from Miss Callingham in person."

My head swam round. It was all like a dream to me. I held my forehead with my hands, and gazed blankly at the Inspector.

"You understand what all this means?" he said interrogatively, leaning forward as he spoke. "You remember the murder?"

"Perfectly," I answered him, trembling all over. "I remember every detail of it. I could describe you exactly all the objects in the room. The Picture it left behind has burned itself into my brain like a flash of lightning!"

The Inspector drew his chair nearer. "Now, Miss Callingham," he said in a very serious voice, "that's a remarkable expression - like a flash of lightning.' Bear in mind, this is a matter of life and death to somebody somewhere. Somebody's neck may depend upon your answers. Will you tell me exactly how much you remember?"

I told him in a few words precisely how the scene had imprinted itself on my memory. I recalled the room, the box, the green wires, the carpet; the man who lay dead in his blood on the floor; the man who stood poised ready to leap from the window. He let me go on unchecked till I'd finished everything I had to say spontaneously. Then he took a photograph from his pocket, which he didn't show me. Looking at it attentively, he asked me questions, one by one, about the different things in the room at the time in very minute detail: Where exactly was the box? How did it stand relatively to the unlighted lamp? What was the position of the pistol on the floor? In which direction was my father's head lying? Though it brought back the Horror to me in a fuller and more terrible form than ever, I answered all his questions to the very best of my ability. I could picture the whole scene like a photograph to myself; and I didn't doubt the object he held in his hand was a photograph of the room as it appeared after the murder. He checked my statements, one by one as I went on, by reference to the photograph, murmuring half to himself now and again: "Yes, yes, exactly so"; "That's right"; "That was so," at each item I mentioned.

At the end of these inquiries, he paused and looked hard at me.

"Now, Miss Callingham," he said again, peering deep into my eyes, "I want you to concentrate your mind very much, not on this Picture you carry so vividly in your own brain, but on the events that went immediately before and after it. Pause long and think. Try hard to remember. And first, you say there was a great flash of light. Now, answer me this: was it one flash alone, or had there been several?"

I stopped and racked my brain. Blank, blank, as usual.

"I can't remember," I faltered out, longing terribly to cry. "I can recall just that one scene, and nothing else in the world before it."

He looked at me fixedly, jotting down a few words in his note-book as he looked. Then he spoke again, still more slowly:

"Now, try once more," he said, with an encouraging air. "You saw this man's back as he was getting out of the window. But can't you remember having seen his face before? Had he a beard? a moustache? what eyes? what nose? Did you see the shot fired? And if so, what sort of person was the man who fired it?"

Again I searched the pigeon-holes of my memory in vain, as I had done a hundred times before by myself.

"It's no use," I cried helplessly, letting my hands drop by my side. "I can't remember a thing, except the Picture. I don't know whether I saw the shot fired or not. I don't know what the murderer looked like in the face. I've told you all I know. I can recall nothing else. It's all a great blank to me."

The Inspector hesitated a moment, as if in doubt what step to take next. Then he drew himself up and said, still more gravely:

"This inability to assist us is really very singular. I had hoped, after Dr. Thornton's report, that we might at last count with some certainty upon arriving at fresh results as to the actual murder. I can see from what you tell me you're a young lady of intelligence - much above the average - and great strength of mind. It's curious your memory should fail you so pointedly just where we stand most in need of its aid. Recollect, nobody else but you ever saw the murderer's face. Now, I'm going to presume you're answering me honestly, and try a bold means to arouse your dormant memory. Look hard, and hark back. - Is that the room you recollect? Is that the picture that still haunts and pursues you?"

He handed me the photograph he held in his fingers. I took it, all on fire. The sight almost made me turn sick with horror. To my awe and amazement, it was indeed the very scene I remembered so well. Only, of course, it was taken from another point of view, and represented things in rather different relative positions to those I figured them in. But it showed my father's body lying dead upon the floor; it showed his poor corpse weltering helpless in its blood; it showed myself, as a girl of eighteen, standing awestruck, gazing on in blank horror at the sight; and in the background, half blurred by the summer evening light, it showed the vague outline of a man's back, getting out of the window. On one side was the door: that formed no part of my mental picture, because it was at my back; but in the photograph it too was indistinct, as if in the very act of being burst open. The details were vague, in part - probably the picture had never been properly focussed; - but the main figures stood out with perfect clearness, and everything in the room was, allowing for the changed point of view, exactly as I remembered it in my persistent mental photograph.

I drew a deep breath.

"That's my Picture," I said, slowly. "But it recalls to me nothing new. I - I don't understand it."

The Inspector stared at me hard once more.

"Do you know," he asked, "how that photograph was produced, and how it came into our possession?"

I trembled violently.

"No, I don't," I answered, reddening. "But - I think it had something to do with the flash like lightning."

The Inspector jumped at those words like a cat upon a mouse.

"Quite right," he cried briskly, as one who at last, after long search, finds a hopeful clue where all seemed hopeless. "It had to do with the flash. The flash produced it. This is a photograph taken by your father's process.... Of course you recollect your father's process?"

He eyed me close. The words, as he spoke them, seemed to call up dimly some faint memory of my pre-natal days - of my First State, as I had learned from the doctors to call it. But his scrutiny made me shrink. I shut my eyes and looked back.

"I think," I said slowly, rummaging my memory half in vain, "I remember something about it. It had something to do with photography, hadn't it?...No, no, with the electric light....I can't exactly remember which. Will you tell me all about it?"

He leaned back in his chair, and, eyeing me all the time with that same watchful glance, began to describe to me in some detail an apparatus which he said my father had devised, for taking instantaneous photographs by the electric light, with a clockwork mechanism. It was an apparatus that let sensitive-plates revolve one after another opposite the lens of a camera; and as each was exposed, the clockwork that moved it produced an electric spark, so as to represent such a series of effects as the successive positions of a horse in trotting. My father, it seemed, was of a scientific turn, and had just perfected this new automatic machine before his sudden death. I listened with breathless interest; for up to that time I had never been allowed to hear anything about my father - anything about the great tragedy with which my second life began. It was wonderful to me even now to be allowed to speak and ask questions on it with anybody. So hedged about had I been all my days with mystery.

As I listened, I saw the Inspector could tell by the answering flash in my eye that his words recalled SOMETHING to me, however vaguely. As he finished, I leant forward, and with a very flushed face, that I could feel myself, I cried, in a burst of recollection:

"Yes, yes. I remember. And the box on the table - the box that's in my mental picture, and is not in the photograph - THAT was the apparatus you've just been describing."

The Inspector turned upon me with a rapidity that fairly took my breath away.

"Well, where are the other ones?" he asked, pouncing down upon me quite fiercely.

"The other WHAT?" I repeated, amazed; for I didn't really understand him.

"Why, the other photographs!" he replied, as if trying to surprise me. "There must have been more, you know. It held six plates. Except for this one, the apparatus, when we found it, was empty."

His manner seemed to crush out the faint spark of recollection that just flickered within me. I collapsed at once. I couldn't stand such brusqueness.

"I don't know what you mean," I answered in despair. "I never saw the plates. I know nothing about them."

CHAPTER IV.

THE STORY OF THE PHOTOGRAPHS

The Inspector scanned me close for a few minutes in silence. He seemed doubtful, suspicious. At last he made a new move. "I believe you, Miss Callingham," he said, more gently. "I can see this train of thought distresses you too much. But I can see, too, our best chance lies in supplying you with independent clues which you may work out for yourself. You must re-educate your memory. You want to know all about this murder, of course. Well, now, look over these papers. They'll tell you in brief what little we know about it. And they may succeed in striking afresh some resonant chord in your memory."

He handed me a book of pasted newspaper paragraphs, interspersed here and there in red ink with little manuscript notes and comments. I began to read it with profound interest. It was so strange for me thus to learn for the first time the history of my own life; for I was quite ignorant as yet of almost everything about my First State, and my father and mother.

The paragraphs told me the whole story of the crime, as far as it was known to the world, from the very beginning. First of all, in the papers, came the bald announcement that a murder had been committed in a country town in Staffordshire; and that the victim was Mr. Vivian Callingham, a gentleman of means, residing in his own house, The Grange, at Woodbury. Mr. Callingham was the inventor of the acmegraphic process. The servants, said the telegram to the London papers, had heard the sound of a pistol-shot, about half-past eight at night, coming from the direction of Mr. Callingham's library. Aroused by the report, they rushed hastily to the spot, and broke open the door, which was locked from within. As they did so, a horrible sight met their astonished eyes. Mr. Callingham's dead body lay extended on the ground, shot right through the heart, and weltering in its life-blood. Miss Callingham stood by his side, transfixed with horror, and mute in her agony. On the floor lay the pistol that had fired the fatal shot. And just as the servants entered, for one second of time, the murderer who was otherwise wholly unknown, was seen to leap from the window into the shrubbery below. The gardener rushed after him, and jumped down at the same spot. But the murderer had disappeared as if by magic. It was conjectured he must have darted down the road at full speed, vaulted the gate, which was usually locked, and made off at a rapid run for the open country. Up to date of going to press, the Telegraph said, he was still at large and had not been apprehended.

That was the earliest account - bald, simple, unvarnished. Then came mysterious messages from the Central Press about the absence of any clue to identify the stranger. He hadn't entered the house by any regular way, it seemed; unless, indeed, Mr. Callingham had brought him home himself and let him in with the latchkey. None of the servants had opened the door that evening to any suspicious character; not a soul had they seen, nor did any of them know a man was with their master in the library. They heard voices, to be sure - voices, loud at times and angry, - but they supposed it was Mr. Callingham talking with his daughter. Till roused by the fatal pistol-shot, the gardener said, they had no cause for alarm. Even the footmarks the stranger might have left as he leaped from the window were obliterated by the prints of the gardener's boots as he jumped hastily after him. The only person who could cast any light upon the mystery at all was clearly Miss Callingham, who was in the room at the moment. But Miss Callingham's mind was completely unhinged for the present by the nervous shock she had received as her father fell dead before her. They must wait a few days till she recovered consciousness, and then they might confidently hope that the murderer would be identified, or at least so described that the police could track him.

After that, I read the report of the coroner's inquest. The facts there elicited added nothing very new to the general view of the case. Only, the servants remarked on examination, there was a strange smell of chemicals in the room when they entered; and the doctors seemed to suggest that the smell might be that of chloroform, mixed with another very powerful drug known to affect the memory. Miss Callingham's present state, they thought, might thus perhaps in part be accounted for.

You can't imagine how curious it was for me to see myself thus impersonally discussed at such a distance of time, or to learn so long after that for ten days or more I had been the central object of interest to all reading England. My name was bandied about without the slightest reserve. I trembled to see how cavalierly the press had treated me.

As I went on, I began to learn more and more about my father. He had made money in Australia, it was said, and had come to live at Woodbury some fourteen years earlier, where my mother had died when I was a child of four; and some accounts said she was a widow of fortune. My father had been interested in chemistry and photography, it seemed, and had lately completed a new invention, the acmegraph, for taking successive photographs at measured intervals of so many seconds by electric light. He was a grave, stern man, the papers said, more feared than loved by his servants and neighbours; but nobody about was known to have a personal grudge against him. On the contrary, he lived at peace with all men. The motive for the murder remained to the end a complete mystery.

On the second morning of the inquest, however, a curious thing happened. The police, it appeared, had sealed up the room where the murder took place, and allowed nobody to enter it till the inquiry was over. But after the jury came round to view the room, the policeman in charge found the window at the back of the house had been recently opened, and the box with the photographic apparatus had been stolen from the library. Till that moment nobody had attached any importance to the presence of this camera. It hadn't even been opened and examined by the police, who had carefully noted everything else in the library. But as soon as the box was missed strange questions began to be asked and conjecturally answered. The police for the first time then observed that though it was half-past eight at night when the murder occurred, and the lamp was not lighted, the witnesses who burst first into the room described all they saw as if they had seen it clearly. They spoke of things as they would be seen in a very bright light, with absolute definiteness. This set up inquiry, and the result of the inquiry was to bring out the fact, which in the excitement of the moment had escaped the notice of all the servants, that as they entered the room and stared about at the murder, the electric flash of the apparatus was actually in operation. But the scene itself had diverted their attention from the minor matter of the light that showed it.

The Inspector had been watching me narrowly as I read these extracts. When I reached that point, he broke in with a word of explanation.

"Well, that put me on the track, you see," he said, leaning forward once more. "I thought to myself, if the light was acting, then the whole apparatus must necessarily have been at work, and the scene as it took place must have been photographed, act by act and step by step, exactly as it happened. At the time the murderer, whoever he was, can't have known the meaning of the flashes. But later, he must have come to learn in some way what the electric light meant, and must have realised, sooner than we did, that therein the box, in the form of six successive negatives of the stages in the crime, was the evidence that would infallibly convict him of this murder." He stroked his moustache thoughtfully. "And to think, too," he went on with a somewhat sheepish air, "we should have had those photographs there in our power all those days and nights, and have let them in the end slip like that through our fingers! To think he should have found it out sooner than we! To think that an amateur like the murderer should have outwitted us!"

"But how do you know," I cried, "there was ever more than one photograph? How do you know this wasn't the only negative?"

"Because," the Inspector answered quickly, pointing to a figure in the corner of the proof, "do you see that six? Well, that tells the tale. Each plate of the series was numbered so in the apparatus. Number six could only fall into focus after numbers one, and two, and three, and four, and five, had first been photographed. We've only got the last - and least useful for our purpose. There must have been five earlier ones, showing every stage of the crime, if only we'd known it."

I was worked up now to a strange pitch of excitement.

"And how did this one come into your possession?" I asked, all breathless. "If you managed to lay your hands on one, why not on all six of them?"

The Inspector drew a long breath.

"Ah, that's the trouble!" he replied, still gazing at me hard. "You see, it was this way. As soon as we found the camera was missing, we came to the conclusion the murderer must have returned to The Grange to fetch it. But it was a large and heavy box, and the only one of its kind as yet manufactured; so, to carry it away in his hands would no doubt have led to instant detection. I concluded, therefore, the man would take off the box entire, so as to prevent the danger of removing the plates on the spot; and as soon as he reached a place of safety in the shrubbery, he'd fling away the camera, either destroying the incriminating negatives then and there or carrying them off with him. The details of the invention had already been explained to me by your father's instrument-maker, who set up the clockwork for him from his own designs; and I knew that the removal of the plates from the box was a delicate, and to some extent a difficult, operation. So I felt sure they could only have been taken out in a place of comparative safety, not far from the house; and I searched the shrubbery carefully, to find the camera."

"And you found it at last?" I asked, unable to restrain my agitation.

"I found it at last," he answered, "near the far end of the grounds, just flung into the deep grass, behind a clump of lilacs. The camera was there intact, but five plates were missing. The sixth, from which the positive you hold in your hand was taken, had got jammed in the mechanism in the effort to remove it. Evidently the murderer had tried to take out the plates in a very great hurry and with trembling hands, as was not unnatural. He had succeeded with five, when the sixth stuck fast in the groove of the clockwork. Just at that moment, as we judged, either an alarm was raised in the rear, or some panic fear seized on him. Probably the fellow judged right that the most incriminating pictures of all had by that time been removed, and that the last would only show his back, if it included him at all, or if he came into focus. Perhaps he had even been able unconsciously to count the flashes at the moment, and knew that before the sixth flash arrived he was on the ledge of the window. At any rate, he clearly gave up the attempt to remove the sixth, and flung the whole apparatus away from him in a sudden access of horror. We guessed as much both from the appearance of the spot where the grass was trampled down, and the way the angle of the camera was imbedded forcibly in the soft ground of the shrubbery."

"And he got away with the rest!" I exclaimed, following it up like a story, but a story in which I was myself an unconscious character.

"No doubt," the Inspector answered, stroking his chin regretfully. "And what's most annoying of all, we've every reason to suppose the fellow stole the things only a few minutes before we actually missed them. For we saw grounds for supposing he jumped away from the spot, and climbed over the wall at the back, cutting his hands as he went with the bottle-glass on the top to prevent intruders. And what makes us think only a very short time must have elapsed between the removal of the plates and the moment we came upon his tracks is this - the blood from his cut hands was still fresh and wet upon the wall when we found it."

"Then you only just missed him!" I exclaimed. "He got off by the skin of his teeth. It's wonderful, when you were so near, you shouldn't have managed to overtake him! One would have thought you must have been able to track him to earth somehow!"

"One would have thought so," the Inspector answered, rather crestfallen. "But policemen, after all, are human like the rest of us. We missed the one chance that might have led to an arrest. And now, what I want to ask you once more is this: Reflecting over what you've heard and read to-day, do you think you can recollect – a very small matter - whether or not there were SEVERAL distinct flashes?"

I shut my eyes once more, and looked hard into the past. Slowly, as I looked, a sort of dream seemed to come over me. I saw it vaguely now, or thought I saw it. Flash, flash, flash, flash. Then the sound of the pistol. Then the Picture, and the Horror, and the awful blank. I opened my eyes again, and told the Inspector so.

"And once more," he went on, in a very insinuating voice. "Shut your eyes again, and look back upon that day. Can't you remember whether or not, just a moment before, you saw the murderer's face by the light of the flashes?"

I shut my eyes and thought. Again the flashes seemed to stand out clear and distinct. But no detail supervened - no face came back to me. I felt it was useless.

"Impossible!" I said shortly. "It only makes my head swim. I can remember no further."

"I see," the Inspector answered. "It's just as Dr. Wade said. Suggest a fact in your past history, and you may possibly remember it; but ask you to recall anything not suggested or already known, and all seems a mere blank to you! You haven't the faintest idea, then, who the murderer was or what he looked like?"

I rose up before him solemnly, and stared him full in the face. I was wrought up by that time to a perfect pitch of excitement and interest.

"I haven't the faintest idea," I answered, feeling myself a woman at last, and realising my freedom; "I know and remember no more of it than you do. But from this moment forth, I shall not rest until I've found him out and tracked him down, and punished him. I shall never let my head rest in peace on my pillow until I've discovered my father's murderer!"

"That's well," the Inspector said sharply, shutting his notes up to go. "If you persevere in that mind, and do as you say, we shall soon get to the bottom of the Woodbury Mystery!"

And even as he spoke a key turned in the front door. I knew it was Aunt Emma, come in from her marketing.

CHAPTER V.

I BECOME A WOMAN

Aunt Emma burst into the room, all horror and astonishment. She looked at the Inspector for a few seconds in breathless indignation; then she broke out in a tone of fiery remonstrance which fairly surprised me:

"What do you mean by this intrusion, sir? How dare you force your way into my house in my absence? How dare you encourage my servants to disobey my orders? How dare you imperil this young lady's health by coming here to talk with her?"

She turned round to me anxiously. I suppose I was very flushed with excitement and surprise.

"My darling child," she cried, growing pale all at once, "Maria should never have allowed him to come inside the door! You should have stopped upstairs! You should have refused to see him! I shall have you ill again on my hands, as before, after this. He'll have undone all the good the last four years have done for you!"

But I was another woman now. I felt it in a moment.

"Auntie dearest," I answered, moving across to her,

and laying my hand on her shoulder to soothe her poor ruffled nerves, "don't be the least alarmed. It's I who'm to blame, and not Maria. I told her to let this gentleman in. He's done me good, not harm. I'm so glad to have been allowed at last to speak freely about it!"

Aunt Emma shook all over, visibly to the naked eye.

"You'll have a relapse, my child!" she exclaimed, half crying, and clinging to me in her terror. "You'll forget all you've learned: you'll go back these four years again! - Leave my house at once, sir! You should never have entered it!"

I stood between them like a statue.

"No, stop here a little longer," I said, waving my hand towards him imperiously. "I haven't yet heard all it's right for me to hear....Auntie, you mistake. I'm a woman at last. I see what everything means. I'm beginning to remember again. For four years that hateful Picture has haunted me night and day. I could never shut my eyes for a minute without seeing it. I've longed to know what it all meant; but whenever I've asked, I've been repressed like a baby. I'm a baby no longer: I feel myself a woman. What the Inspector here has told me already, half opens my eyes: I must have them opened altogether now. I can't stop at this point. I'm going back to Woodbury."

Aunt Emma clung to me still harder in a perfect agony of passionate terror.

"To Woodbury, my darling!" she cried. "Going back! Oh, Una, it'll kill you!"

"I think not," the Inspector answered, with a very quiet smile. "Miss Callingham has recovered, I venture to say, far more profoundly than you imagine. This repression, our medical adviser tells us, has been bad for her. If she's allowed to visit freely the places connected with her earlier life, it may all return again to her; and the ends of Justice may thus at last be served for us. I notice already one hopeful symptom: Miss Callingham speaks of going back to Woodbury."

Aunt Emma looked up at him, horrified. All her firmness was gone now.

"It's YOU who've put this into her head!" she exclaimed, in a ferment of horror. "She'd never thought of it herself. You've made her do it!"

"On the contrary, auntie," I answered, feeling my ground grow surer under me every moment as I spoke, "this gentleman has never even by the merest hint suggested such an idea to my mind. It occurred to me quite spontaneously. I MUST find out now who was my father's murderer! All the Inspector has told me seems to arouse in my brain some vague, forgotten chords. It brings back to me faint shadows. I feel sure if I went to Woodbury I should remember much more. And then, you must see for yourself, there's another reason, dear, that ought to make me go. Nobody but I ever saw the murderer's face. It's a duty imposed upon me from without, as it were, never to rest again in peace till I've recognised him."

Aunt Emma collapsed into an easy-chair. Her face was deadly pale. Her ringers trembled.

"If you go, Una," she cried, playing nervously with her

gloves, "I must go with you too! I must take care of you: I must watch over you!"

I took her quivering hand in mine and stroked it gently. It was a soft and delicate white little hand, all marked inside with curious ragged scars that I'd known and observed ever since I first knew her. I held it in silence for a minute. Somehow I felt our positions were reversed to-day. This interview had suddenly brought out what I know now to be my own natural and inherent character - self-reliant, active, abounding in initiative. For four years I had been as a child in her hands, through mere force of circumstances. My true self came out now and asserted its supremacy.

"No, dear," I said, soothing her cheek; "I shall go alone. I shall try what I can discover and remember myself without any suggestion or explanation from others. I want to find out how things really stand. I shall set to work on my own account to unravel this mystery."

"But how can you manage things by yourself?" Aunt Emma exclaimed, wringing her hands despondently. "A girl of your age! without even a maid! and all alone in the world! I shall be afraid to let you go. Dr. Wade won't allow it."

I drew myself up very straight, and realised the position.

"Aunt Emma," I said plainly, in a decided voice, "I'm a full-grown woman, over twenty-one years of age, mistress of my own acts, and no longer a ward of yours. I can do as I like, and neither Dr. Wade nor anybody else can prevent me. He may ADVICE me not to go: he has no power to ORDER me. I'm my father's heiress, and a person of independent means. I've been a cipher too long. From to-day I take my affairs wholly into my own hands. I 'll go round at once and see your lawyer, your banker, your agent, your tradesmen, and tell them that henceforth I draw my own rents, I receive my own dividends, I pay my own bills, I keep my own banking account. And to-morrow or the next day I set out for Woodbury."

The Inspector turned to Aunt Emma with a demonstrative smile.

"There, you see for. yourself," he said, well pleased, "what this interview has done for her!"

But Aunt Emma only drew back, wrung her hands again in impotent despair, and stared at him blankly like a wounded creature.

The Inspector took up his hat to leave. I followed him out to the door, and shook hands with him cordially. The burden felt lighter on my shoulders already. For four long years that mystery had haunted me day and night, as a thing impenetrable, incomprehensible, not even to be inquired about. The mere sense that I might now begin to ask what it meant seemed to make it immediately less awful and less burdensome to me.

When I returned to the drawing-room, Aunt Emma sat there on the sofa, crying silently, the very picture of misery.

"Una," she said, without even raising her eyes to mine, "the man may have done as he says: he may have restored you your mind again; but what's that to me?

He's lost me my child, my darling, my daughter!"

I stooped down and kissed her. Dear, tender-hearted auntie! she had always been very good to me. But I knew I was right, for all that, in becoming a woman, - in asserting my years, my independence, my freedom, my duty. To have shirked it any longer would have been sheer cowardice. So I just kissed her silently, and went up to my own room - to put on my brown hat, and go out to the banker's.

From that moment forth, one fierce desire in life alone possessed me. The brooding mystery that enveloped my life ceased to be passive, and became an active goad, as it were, to push me forward incessantly on my search for the runaway I was the creature of a fixed idea. A fiery energy spurred me on all my time. I was determined now to find out my father's murderer. I was determined to shake off the atmosphere of doubt and forgetfulness. I was determined to recall those first scenes of my life that so eluded my memory.

Yet, strange to say, it was rather a burning curiosity and a deep sense of duty that urged me on, than anything I could properly call affection - still less, revenge or malice. I didn't remember my father as alive at all: the one thing I could recollect about him was the ghastly look of that dead body, stretched at full length on the library floor, with its white beard all dabbled in the red blood that clotted it. It was abstract zeal for the discovery of the truth that alone pushed me on. This search became to me henceforth an end and aim in itself. It stood out, as it were, visibly in the imperative mood: "go here;" "go there;" "do this;" "try that;" "leave no stone unturned anywhere till you've tracked down the murderer!" Those were the voices that now incessantly though inaudibly pursued me.

Next day I spent in preparations for my departure. I would hunt up Woodbury now, though fifty Aunt Emma's held their gentle old faces up in solemn warning against me. The day after that again, I set out on my task. The pull was hard. I had taken my own affairs entirely into my own hands by that time, and had provided myself with money for a long stay at Woodbury. But it was the very first railway journey I could ever remember to have made alone; and I confess, when I found myself seated all by myself in a first-class carriage, with no friend beside me, my resolution for a moment almost broke down again. It was so terrible to feel oneself boxed up there for an hour or two alone, with that awful Picture staring one in the face all the time from every fence and field and wall and hoarding. It obliterated Fry's Cocoa; it fixed itself on the yellow face of Colman's Mustard.

I went by Liverpool Street, and drove across to Paddington. I had never, to my knowledge, been in London before: and it was all so new to me. But Liverpool Street was even newer to me than Paddington, I noticed. A faint sense of familiarity seemed to hang about the Great Western line. And that was not surprising, I thought, as I turned it over; for, of course, in the old days, when we lived at Woodbury, I must often have come down from town that way with my father. Yet I remembered nothing of it all definitely; the most I could say was that I seemed dimly to recollect having been there before - though when or where or how, I hadn't the faintest notion.

I was early at Paddington. The refreshment room somehow failed to attract me. I walked up and down the platform, waiting for my train. As I did so, a boy pasted a poster on a board: it was the contents-sheet of one of the baser little Society papers. Something strange in it caught my eye. I looked again in amazement. Oh, great heavens! what was this in big flaring letters?

"MISS UNA CALLINGHAM AND THE WOODBURY MYSTERY! Is SHE SCREENING THE MURDERER? A POSSIBLE EXPLANATION!"

The words took my breath away. They were too horrible to realise. I positively couldn't speak. I went up to the bookstall, laid down my penny without moving my lips, and took the paper in my hand in tremulous silence.

I dared not open it there and then, I confess. I waited till I was in the train, and on my way to Woodbury.

When I did so, it was worse, even worse than my fears. The article was short, but it was very hateful. It said nothing straight out - the writer had evidently the fear of the law of libel before his eyes as he wrote, - but it hinted and insinuated in a detestable undertone the most vile innuendoes. A Treasury Doctor and a Police Inspector, it said, had lately examined Miss Callingham again, and found her intellect in every respect perfectly normal, except that she couldn't remember the face of her father's murderer. Now, this was odd, because, you see, Miss Callingham was in the room at the moment the shot was fired; and, alone in the world, Miss Callingham had seen the face of the man who fired it. Who was that man? and why was he there, unknown to the servants, in a room with nobody but Mr. Callingham and his daughter? A correspondent (who preferred to guard his incognito) had suggested in this matter some very searching questions: Could the young man - for it was allowed he was young - have been there with Miss Callingham when Mr. Callingham entered? Could he have been on terms of close intimacy with the heroine of The Grange Mystery, who was a young lady - as all the world knew from her photographs - of great personal attractiveness, and who was also the heiress to a considerable property? Could he have been there, then, by appointment, without the father's knowledge? Was this the common case of a clandestine assignation? Could the father have returned to the house unexpectedly, at an inopportune moment, and found his daughter there, closeted with a stranger - perhaps with a man who had already, for sufficient grounds, been forbidden the premises? Such things might be, in this world that we live in: he would be a bold man who would deny them categorically. Could an altercation have arisen on the father's return, and the fatal shot have been fired in the ensuing scuffle? And could the young lady then have feigned this curious relapse into that Second State we had all heard so much about, for no other reason than to avoid giving evidence at a trial for murder against her guilty lover?

These were suggestions that deserved the closest consideration of the Authorities charged with the repression of crime. Was it not high time that the inquest on Mr. Callingham's body should be formally reopened, and that the young lady, now restored (as we gathered) to her own seven senses, should be closely interrogated by trained legal cross-examiners?

I laid down the paper with a burning face. I learned now, for the first time, how closely my case had been watched, how eagerly my every act and word had been canvassed. It was hateful to think of my photograph having been exposed in every London shop-window, and of anonymous slanderers being permitted to indite such scandal as this about an innocent woman. But, at any rate, it had the effect of sealing my fate. If I meant even before to probe this mystery to the bottom, I felt now no other course was possibly open to me. For the sake of my own credit, for the sake of my own good fame, I must find out and punish my father's murderer.

CHAPTER VI.

RELIVING MY LIFE

Often, as you walk down a street, a man or woman passes you by. You look up at them and say to yourself, "I seem to know that face"; but you can put no name to it, attach to it no definite idea, no associations of any sort. That was just how Woodbury struck me when I first came back to it. The houses, the streets, the people, were in a way familiar; yet I could no more have found my way alone from the station to The Grange than I could find my way alone from here to Kamschatka.

So I drove up first in search of lodgings. At the station even several people had bowed or shaken hands with me respectfully as I descended from the train. They came up as if they thought I must recognise them at once: there was recognition in their eyes; but when they met my blank stare, they seemed to remember all about it, and merely murmured in strange tones:

"Good-morning, miss! So you're here: glad to see you've come back again at last to Woodbury."

This reception dazzled me. It was so strange, so uncanny. I was glad to get away in a fly by myself, and to be driven to lodgings in the clean little High Street.

Grant Allen

For to me, it wasn't really "coming back" at all: it was coming to a strange town, where everyone knew me, and *I* knew nobody.

"You'd like to go to Jane's, of course," the driver said to me with a friendly nod as he reached the High Street: and not liking to confess my forgetfulness of Jane, I responded with warmth that Jane's would, no doubt, exactly suit me.

We drew up at the door of a neat little house. The driver rang the bell.

"Miss Una's here," he said, confidentially; "and she's looking for lodgings."

It was inexpressibly strange and weird to me, this one-sided recognition, this unfamiliar familiarity: it gave me a queer thrill of the supernatural that I can hardly express to you. But I didn't know what to do, when a kindly-faced, middle-aged English upper-class servant rushed out at me, open-armed, and hugging me hard to her breast, exclaimed with many loud kisses:

"Miss Una, Miss Una! So it's YOU, dear; so it is! Then you've come back at last to us!"

I could hardly imagine what to say or do. The utmost I could assert with truth was, Jane's face wasn't exactly and entirely in all ways unfamiliar to me. Yet I could see Jane herself was so unfeignedly delighted to see me again, that I hadn't the heart to confess I'd forgotten her very existence. So I took her two hands in mine - since friendliness begets friendliness - and holding her off a little way, for fear the kisses should be repeated, I said to her very gravely:

"You see, Jane, since those days I've had a terrible shock, and you can hardly expect me to remember anything. It's all like a dream to me. You must forgive me if I don't recall it just at once as I ought to do."

"Oh! yes, miss," Jane answered, holding my hands in her delight and weeping volubly. "We've read about all that, of course, in the London newspapers. But there, I'm glad anyhow you remembered to come and look for my lodgings. I think I should just have sat down and cried if they told me Miss Una'd come back to Woodbury, and never so much as asked to see me."

I don't think I ever felt so like a hypocrite in my life before. But I realised at least that even if Jane's lodgings were discomfort embodied, I must take them and stop in them, while I remained there, now. Nothing else was possible. I COULDN'T go elsewhere.

Fortunately, however, the rooms turned out to be as neat as a new pin, and as admirably kept as any woman in England could keep them. I gathered from the very first, of course, that Jane had been one of the servants at The Grange in the days of my First State; and while I drank my cup of tea, Jane herself came in and talked volubly to me, disclosing to me, parenthetically, the further fact that she was the parlour-maid at the time of my father's murder. That gave me a clue to her identity. Then she was the witness Greenfield who gave evidence at the inquest! I made a mental note of that, and determined to look up what she'd said to the coroner, in the book of extracts the Inspector gave me, as soon as I got alone in my bedroom that evening.

After dinner, however, Jane came in again, with the freedom of an old servant, and talked to me much about the Woodbury Mystery. Gradually, as time went on that night, though I remembered nothing definite of myself about her, the sense of familiarity and friendliness came home to me more vividly. The appropriate emotion seemed easier to rouse, I observed, than the intellectual memory. I knew Jane and I had been on very good terms, some time, some-where. I talked with her easily, for I had a consciousness of companionship.

By-and-by, without revealing to her how little I could recollect about her own personality, I confessed to Jane, by slow degrees, that the whole past was still gone utterly from my shattered memory. I told her I knew nothing except the Picture and the facts it comprised; and to show her just how small that knowledge really was, I showed her (imprudently enough) the photograph the Inspector had left with me.

Jane looked at it long and slowly, with tears in her eyes. Then she said at last, after a deep pause, in a very hushed voice:

"Why, how did you get this? It wasn't put in the papers."

"No," I answered quietly, "it wasn't put in the papers. For reasons of their own, the police kept it unpublished."

Jane gazed at the proof still closer. "They oughtn't to have done that," she said.

"They ought to have sent it out everywhere broadcast - so that anybody who knew the man could tell him by his back."

That seemed to me such obvious good sense that I wondered to myself the police hadn't thought long since of it; but I supposed they had some good ground of their own for holding it all this time in their own possession.

Jane went on talking to me still for many minutes about the scene:

"Ah, yes; that was just how he lay, poor dear gentleman! And the book on the chair, too! Well, did you ever in your life see anything so like! And to think it was taken all by itself, as one might say, by magic. But there! your poor papa was a wonderful clever man. Such things as he used to invent! Such ideas and such machines! We were sorry for him, though we always thought, to be sure, he was dreadful severe with you, Miss Una. Such a gentleman to have his own way, too - so cold and reserved like. But one mustn't talk nothing but good about the dead, they say. And if he was a bit hard, he was more than hard treated for it in the end, poor gentleman!"

It interested me to get these half side-lights on my father's character. Knowing nothing of him, as I did, save the solitary fact that he was the white-haired gentleman I saw dead in my Picture, I naturally wanted to learn as much as I could from this old servant of ours as to the family conditions.

"Then you thought him harsh, in the servants'-hall?" I said tentatively to Jane. "You thought him hard and unbending?"

"Well, there, Miss," Jane ran on, putting a cushion to my back tenderly - it was strange to be the recipient of so much delicate attention from a perfect stranger, - "not exactly what you'd call harsh to us ourselves, you know: he was a good master enough, as long as one did what was ordered, though he was a little bit fidgetty. But to you, we all thought he was always rather hard. People said so in Woodbury. And yet, in a way, I don't know how it was, he always seemed more'n half afraid of you. He was careful about your health, and spoiled and petted you for that; yet he was always pulling you up, you know, and looking after what you did: and for one thing, I remember, there's many a time you were sent to bed when you were a good big girl for nothing on earth else but because he heard you talking to us in the hall about Australia."

"Talking to you about Australia!" I cried, pricking my ears. "Why, what harm was there in that? Why on earth didn't he want me to talk about Australia?"

"Ah! what harm indeed?" Jane echoed blandly. "That's what we often used to say among ourselves downstairs. But Mr. Callingham, he was always that way, miss - so strict and particular. He said he'd forbidden you to say a word to anybody about that confounded country; and you must do as you were told. He seemed to have a grudge against Australia, though it was there he made his money. And he always would have his own way, your father would."

While she spoke, I looked hard at the white head in the photograph. Even as I did so, a thought occurred to me that had never occurred before. Both in my mental Picture, and in looking at the photograph when I saw it first, the feeling that was uppermost in my mind was not sorrow, but horror. I didn't think with affection and regret and a deep sense of bereavement about my father's murder. The emotional accompaniment that had stamped itself upon the very fibre of my soul, was not pain but awe. I think my main feeling was a feeling that a foul crime had taken place in the house, not a feeling that I had lost a very dear and near relative. Rightly or wrongly, I drew from this the inference, which Jane's gossip confirmed, that I had probably rather feared than loved my father.

It was strange to be reduced to such indirect evidence on such a point as that; but it was all I could get, and I had to be content with it.

Jane, leaning over my shoulder, looked hard at the photograph too. I could see her eyes were fixed on the back of the man who was seen disappearing through the open window. He was dressed like a gentleman, in knickerbockers and jacket, as far as one could judge; for the evening light rather blurred that part of the picture. One hand was just waved, palm open, behind him. Jane regarded it hard. Then she gave an odd little start:

"Why, just look at that hand!" she cried, with a tremor of surprise. "Don't you see what it is? Don't you think it's a woman's?"

I gazed back at her incredulously.

"Impossible," I answered, shaking my head. "It belongs as clear as day to the man you see in the photograph. How on earth could his hand be a woman's then, I'd like to know? I can see the shirt-cuff."

"Why, yes," Jane answered, with simple common-sense: "it's DRESSED like a man, of course, and it's a man to look at; but the hand's a woman's, as true as I'm standing here. Why mightn't a woman dress in a man's suit on purpose? And perhaps it was just because they were so sure it was a man as did it, that the police has gone wrong so long in trying to find the murderer."

I looked hard at the hand myself. Then I shut my eyes, and thought of the corresponding object in my mental Picture. The result fairly staggered me. The impression in each case was exactly the same. It was a soft and delicate hand, very white and womanlike. But was it really a woman's? I couldn't feel quite sure in my own mind about that; but the very warning Jane gave me seemed to me a most useful one. It would be well, after all, to keep one's mind sedulously open to every possible explanation, and to take nothing for granted as to the murderer's personality.

CHAPTER VII.

THE GRANGE AT WOODBURY

I stopped for three weeks in Jane's lodgings; and before the end of that time, Jane and I had got upon the most intimate footing. It was partly her kindliness that endeared her to me, and her constant sense of continuity with the earlier days which I had quite forgotten; but it was partly too, I felt sure, a vague revival within my own breast of a familiarity that had long ago subsisted between us. I was coming to myself again, on one side of my nature. Day by day I grew more certain that while facts had passed away from me, appropriate emotions remained vaguely present. Among the Woodbury people that I met, I recognised none to say that I knew them; but I knew almost at first sight that I liked this one and disliked that one. And in every case alike, when I talked the matter over afterwards with Jane, she confirmed my suspicion that in my First State I had liked or disliked just those persons respectively. My brain was upset, but my heart remained precisely the same as ever.

On my second morning I went up to The Grange with her. The house was still unlet. Since the day of the murder, nobody cared to live in it. The garden and shrubbery had been sadly neglected: Jane took me out of the way as we walked up the path, to show me the place where the photographic apparatus had been found embedded in the grass, and where the murderer had cut his hands getting over the wall in his frantic agitation. The wall was pretty high and protected with bottle-glass. I guessed he must have been tall to scramble over it. That seemed to tell against Jane's crude idea that a woman might have done it.

But when I said so to Jane, she met me at once with the crushing reply: "Perhaps it wasn't the same person that came back for the box." I saw she was right again. I had jumped at a conclusion. In cases like this, one must leave no hypothesis untried, jump at no conclusions of any sort. Clearly, that woman ought to have been made a detective.

As I entered the house the weird sense of familiarity that pursued me throughout rose to a very high pitch. I couldn't fairly say, indeed, that I remembered the different rooms. All I could say with certainty was that I had seen them before. To this there were three exceptions - the three that belonged to my Second State - the library, my bedroom, and the hall and staircase. The first was indelibly printed on my memory as a component part of the Picture, and I found my recollection of every object in the room almost startling in its correctness. Only, there was an alcove on one side that I'd quite forgotten, and I saw why most clearly. I stood with my back to it as I looked at the Picture. The other two bits I remembered as the room in which I had had my first great illness, and the passage down which I had been carried or helped when I was taken to Aunt Emma's.

I had begun to recognise now that the emotional impression made upon me by people and things was the only sure guide I still possessed as to their connection or association with my past history. And the rooms at The Grange had each in this way some distinctive characteristic. The library, of course, was the chief home of the Horror which had hung upon my spirit even during the days when I hardly knew in any intelligible sense the cause of it. But the drawing-room and dining-room both produced upon my mind a vague consciousness of constraint. I was dimly aware of being ill at ease and uncomfortable in them. My own bedroom, on the contrary, gave me a pleasant feeling of rest and freedom and security: while the servants'-hall and the kitchen seemed perfect paradises of liberty.

"Ah! many's the time, miss," Jane said with a sigh, looking over at the empty grate, "you'd come down here to make cakes or puddings, and laugh and joke like a child with Mary an' me. I often used to say to Emily - her as was cook here before Ellen Smith, - 'Miss Una's never so happy as when she's down here in the kitchen.' And 'That's true what you say,' says Emily to me, many a time and often."

That was exactly the impression left upon my own mind. I began to conclude, in a dim, formless way, that my father must have been a somewhat stern and unsympathetic man; that I had felt constrained and uncomfortable in his presence upstairs, and had often been pleased to get away from his eye to the comparative liberty and ease of my own room or of the maid-servants' quarters.

At last, in the big attic that had once been the nursery, I paused and looked at Jane. A queer sensation came over me.

"Jane," I said slowly, hardly liking to frame the words, "there's something strange about this room. He wasn't cruel to me, was he?"

"Oh! no, miss," Jane answered promptly. "He wasn't never what you might call exactly cruel. He was a very good father, and looked after you well; but he was sort of stern and moody-like - would have his own way, and didn't pay no attention to fads and fancies, he called 'em. When you were little, many's the time he sent you up here for punishment - disobedience and such like."

I took out the photograph and tried, as it were, to think of my father as alive and with his eyes open. I couldn't remember the eyes. Jane told me they were blue; but I think what she said was the sort of impression the face produced upon me. A man not unjust or harsh in his dealings with myself, but very strong and masterful. A man who would have his own way in spite of anybody. A father who ruled his daughter as a vessel of his making, to be done as he would with, and be moulded to his fashion.

Still, my visit to The Grange resulted in the end in casting very little light upon the problem before me. It pained and distressed me greatly, but it brought no new elements of the case into view: at best, it only familiarised me with the scene of action of the tragedy. The presence of the alcove was the one fresh feature. Nothing recalled to me as yet in any way the murderer's features. I racked my brain in vain; no fresh image came up in it. I could recollect nothing about the man or his antecedents.

I almost began to doubt that I would ever succeed in

reconstructing my past, when even the sight of the home in which I had spent my childish days suggested so few new thoughts or ideas to me.

For a day or two after that I rested at Jane's, lest I should disturb my brain too much. Then I called once more on the doctor who had made the post mortem on my father, and given evidence at the inquest, to see if anything he could say might recall my lapsed memory.

The moment he came into the room - a man about fifty, close-shaven and kindly-looking - I recognised him at once, and held out my hand to him frankly. He surveyed me from head to foot with a good medical stare, and then wrung my hand in return with extraordinary warmth and effusion. I could see at once he retained a most pleasing recollection of my First State, and was really glad to see me.

"What, you remember me then, Una!" he cried, with quite fatherly delight. "You haven't forgotten me, my dear, as you've forgotten all the rest, haven't you?"

It was startling to be called by one's Christian name like that, and by a complete stranger, too; but I was getting quite accustomed now to these little incongruities.

"Oh, yes; I remember you perfectly," I answered, half-grieved to distress him, "though I shouldn't have known your name, and didn't expect to see you. You're the doctor who attended me in my first great illness - the illness with which my present life began - just after the murder."

He drew back, a little crestfallen.

"Then that's all you recollect, is it?" he asked. "You don't remember me before, dear? Not Dr. Marten, who used to take you on his knee when you were a tiny little girl, and bring you lollipops from town, to the great detriment of your digestion, and get into rows with your poor father for indulging you and spoiling you? You must surely remember me?"

I shook my head slowly. I was sorry to disappoint him; but it was necessary before all things to get at the bare truth.

"I'm afraid not," I answered. "Do please forgive me! You must have read in the papers, like everybody else, of the very great change that has so long come over me. Bear in mind, I can't remember anything at all that occurred before the murder. That first illness is to me the earliest recollection of childhood."

He gazed across at me compassionately.

"My poor child," he said in a low voice, like a very affectionate friend, "it's much better so. You have been mercifully spared a great deal of pain. Una, when I first saw you at The Grange after your father's death, I thanked heaven you had been so seized. I thanked heaven the world had become suddenly a blank to you. I prayed hard you might never recover your senses again, or at least your memory. And now that you're slowly returned to life once more, against all hope or fear, I'm heartily glad it's in this peculiar way. I'm heartily glad all the past's blotted out for you. You can't understand that, my child? Ah, no, very likely not. But I think it's much best for you, all your first life should be wholly forgotten." He paused for a second. Then he added slowly: "If you remembered it all, the sense of the tragedy would be far more acute and poignant even than at present."

"Perhaps so," I said resolutely; "but not the sense of mystery. It's THAT that appals me so! I'd rather know the truth than be so wrapped up in the incomprehensible."

He looked at me pityingly once more.

"My poor child," he said, in the same gentle and fatherly voice, "you don't wholly understand. It doesn't all come home to you. I can see clearly, from what Inspector Wolferstan told me, after his visit to you the other day - "

I broke in, in surprise.

"Inspector Wolferstan!" I cried. "Then he came down here to see you, did he?"

It was horrible to find how all my movements were discussed and chronicled.

"Yes, he came down here to see me and talk things over," Dr. Marten went on, as calmly as if it were mere matter of course. "And I could see from what he said you were still spared much. For instance, you remember it all only as an event that happened to an old man with a long white beard. You don't fully realise, except intellectually, that it was your own father. You're saved, as a daughter, the misery and horror of thinking and feeling it was your father who lay dead there."

"That's quite true," I answered. "I admit that I can't feel

it all as deeply as I ought. But none the less, I've come down here to make a violent effort. Let it cost what it may, I must get at the truth. I wanted to see whether the sight of The Grange and of Woodbury may help me to recall the lost scenes in my memory."

To my immense surprise, Dr. Marten rose from his seat, and standing up before me in a perfect agony of what seemed like terror, half mixed with affection, exclaimed in a very earnest and resolute voice:

"Oh, Una, my child, whatever you do - I beg of you - I implore you - don't try to recall the past at all! Don't attempt it! Don't dream of it!"

"Why not?" I cried, astonished. "Surely it's my duty to try and find out my father's murderer!"

Instead of answering me, he looked about him for half a minute in suspense, as if doubtful what next to do or to say. Then he walked across with great deliberation to the door of the room, and locked and double-locked it with furtive alarm, as I interpreted his action.

So terrified did he seem, indeed, that for a moment the idea occurred to me in a very vague way - Was I talking with the murderer? Had the man who himself committed the crime conducted the post mortem, and put Justice off the scent? And was I now practically at the mercy of the criminal I was trying to track down? The thought for a second or two made me feel terribly uncomfortable. But I glanced at his back and at his hands, and reassured myself. That broad, short man was not the slim figure of my Picture and of the photograph. Those large red hands were not the originals of the small and delicate white palm just displayed at the back in both those strange documents of the mysterious murder.

The doctor came over again, and drew his chair close to mine.

"Una, my child," he said slowly, "I love you very much, as if you were my own daughter. I always loved you and admired you, and was sorry - oh, so sorry! - for you. You've quite forgotten who I am; but I've not forgotten you. Take what I say as coming from an old friend, from one who loves you and has your interest at heart. For heaven's sake, I implore you, my child, make no more inquiries. Try to forget - not to remember. If you do recollect, you'll be sorry in the end for it."

"Why so?" I asked, amazed, yet somehow feeling in my heart I could trust him implicitly. "Why should the knowledge of the true circumstances of the case make me more unhappy than I am at present?"

He gazed harder at me than ever.

"Because," he replied in slow tones, weighing each word as he spoke, "you may find that the murder was committed by some person or persons you love or once loved very much indeed. You may find it will rend your very heart-strings to see that person or those persons punished. You may find the circumstances were wholly otherwise than you imagine them to be.... Let sleeping dogs lie, my dear. Without your aid, nothing more can be done. Don't trouble yourself to put the blood-hounds on the track of some unhappy creature who might otherwise escape. Don't rake it all up afresh. Bury it - bury it - bury it!"

He spoke so earnestly that he filled me with vague alarm.

"Dr. Marten," I said solemnly, "answer me just one question. Do you know who was the murderer?"

"No, no!" he exclaimed, starting once more. "Thank heaven, I can't tell you that! I don't know. I know nothing. Nobody on earth knows but the two who were present on the night of the murder, I feel sure. And of those two, one's unknown, and the other has forgotten."

"But you suspect who he is?" I put in, probing the secret curiously.

He trembled visibly.

"I suspect who he is," he replied, after a moment's hesitation. "But I have never communicated, and will never communicate, my suspicions to anybody, not even to you. I will only say this: the person whom I suspect is one with whom you may now have forgotten all your past relations, but whom you would be sorry to punish if you recovered your memory. I formed a strong opinion at the time who that person was. I formed it from the nature and disposition of the wound, and the arrangement of the objects in the room when I was called in to see your father's body."

"And you never said so at the inquest!" I cried, indignant.

He looked at me hard again. Then he spoke in a very slow and earnest voice:

"For your sake, Una, and for the sake of your affections, I held my peace," he said. "My dear, the suspicion was but a very slender one: I had nothing to go upon. And why should I have tried to destroy your happiness?"

That horrible article in the penny Society paper came back to my mind once more with hideous suggestiveness. I turned to him almost fiercely.

"So far as you know, Dr. Marten," I asked, "was I ever in love? Had I ever an admirer? Was I ever engaged to anyone?"

He shrugged his shoulders and smiled a sort of smile of relief.

"How should I know?" he answered. "Admirers? - yes, dozens of them; I was one myself. Lovers? - who can say? But I advise you not to push the inquiry further."

I questioned him some minutes longer, but could get nothing more from him. Then I rose to go.

"Dr. Marten," I said firmly, "if I remember all, and if it wrings my heart to remember, I tell you I will give up that man to justice all the same! I think I know myself well enough to know this much at least, that I never, never could stoop either to love or to screen a man who could commit such a foul and dastardly crime as this one."

He took my hand fervently, raised it with warmth to his lips and kissed it twice over.

"My dear," he said, with tears dropping down his

gentle old cheeks, "this is a very great mystery - a terrible mystery. But I know you speak the truth. I can see you mean it. Therefore, all the more earnestly do I beg and beseech you, go away from Woodbury at once, and as long as you live think no more about it."

CHAPTER VIII.

A VISION OF DEAD YEARS

The interview with Dr. Marten left me very much disquieted. But it wasn't the only disquieting thing that occurred at Woodbury. Before I left the place I happened to go one day into Jane's own little sitting-room. Jane was anxious I should see it - she wanted me to know all her house, she said, for the sake of old times: and for the sake of those old times that I couldn't remember, but when I knew she'd been kind to me, I went in and looked at it.

There was nothing very peculiar about Jane's little sitting-room: just the ordinary English landlady's parlour. You know the type: - square table in the middle; bright blue vases on the mantelpiece; chromo-lithograph from the Illustrated London News on the wall; rickety whatnot with glass-shaded wax-flowers in the recess by the window. But over in one corner I chanced to observe a framed photograph of early execution, which hung faded and dim there. Perhaps it was because my father was such a scientific amateur; but photography, I found out in time, struck the key-note of my history in every chapter. I didn't know why, but this particular picture attracted me strangely. It came from The Grange, Jane told me: she'd hunted it out in the attic over the front bedroom after the house was shut up. It belonged to a lot of my father's early attempts that were locked in a box there. "He'd always been trying experiments and things," she said, "with photography, poor gentleman."

Faded and dim as it was, the picture riveted my eyes at once by some unknown power of attraction. I gazed at it long and earnestly. It represented a house of colonial aspect, square, wood-built, and verandah-girt, standing alone among strange trees whose very names and aspects were then unfamiliar to me, but which I nowadays know to be Australian eucalyptuses. On the steps of the verandah sat a lady in deep mourning. A child played by her side, and a collie dog lay curled up still and sleepy in the foreground. The child, indeed, stirred no chord of any sort in my troubled brain; but my heart came up into my mouth so at sight of the lady, that I said to myself all at once in my awe, "That must surely be my mother!"

The longer I looked at it, the more was I convinced I must have judged aright. Not indeed that in any true sense I could say I remembered her face or figure: I was so young when she died, according to everybody's account, that even if I'd remained in my First State I could hardly have retained any vivid recollection of her. But both lady and house brought up in me once more to some vague degree that strange consciousness of familiarity I had noticed at The Grange: and what was odder still, the sense of wont seemed even more marked in the Australian cottage than in the case of the house which all probability would have inclined one beforehand to think I must have remembered better. If this was indeed my earliest home, then I seemed to recollect it far more readily than my later one.

I turned trembling to Jane, hardly daring to frame the question that rose first to my lips.

"Is that - my mother?" I faltered out slowly.

But there Jane couldn't help me. She'd never seen the lady, she said.

"When first I come to The Grange, miss, you see, your mother'd been buried a year; there was only you and Mr. Callingham in family. And I never saw that photograph, neither, till I picked it out of the box locked up in the attic. The little girl might be you, like enough, when you look at it sideways; and yet again it mightn't. But the lady I don't know. I never saw your mother."

So I was fain to content myself with pure conjecture.

All day long, however, the new picture haunted me almost as persistently as the old one.

That night I went to sleep fast, and slept for some hours heavily. I woke with a start. I had been dreaming very hard. And my dream was peculiarly clear and lifelike. Never since the first night of my new life - the night of the murder - had I dreamed such a dream, or seen dead objects so vividly. It came out in clear colours, like the terrible Picture that had haunted me so long. And it affected me strangely. It was a scene, rather than a dream - a scene, as at the theatre; but a scene in which I realised and recognised everything.

I stood on the steps of a house - a white wooden house, with a green-painted verandah - the very house I had seen that afternoon in the faded photograph in Jane's little sitting-room. But I didn't think of it at first as the house in the old picture: I thought of it as home - our own place - the cottage. The steps seemed to me very high, as in childish recollection. A lady walked about on the verandah and called to me: a lady in a white gown, like the lady in the photograph, only younger and prettier, and dressed much more daintily. But I didn't think of her as that either: I called her mamma to myself: I looked up into her face, oh, ever so much above me: I must have been very small indeed when that picture first occurred to me. There was a gentleman, too, in a white linen coat, who pinched my mamma's ear, and talked softly and musically. But I didn't think of him quite so: I knew he was my papa: I played about his knees, a little scampering child, and looked up in his face, and teased him and laughed at him. My papa looked down at me, and called me a little kitten, and rolled me over on my back, and fondled me and laughed with me. There were trees growing all about, big trees with long grey leaves: the same sort of trees as the ones in the photograph. But I didn't remember that at first: in my dream, and in the first few minutes of my waking thought, I knew them at once as the big blue-gum-trees.

I awoke in the midst of it: and the picture persisted.

Then, with a sudden burst of intuition, the truth flashed upon me all at once. My dream was no mere dream, but a revelation in my sleep. It was my intellect working unconsciously and spontaneously in an automatic condition. For the very first time in my life, since the night of the murder, I had really REMEMBERED something that occurred before it.

This was a scene of my First State. In all probability it

was my earliest true childish recollection.

I sat up in bed, appalled. I dared not call aloud or ring for Jane to come to me. But if I'd seen a ghost, it could hardly have affected me more profoundly than this ghost of my own dead life thus brought suddenly back to me. Gazing away across some illimitable vista of dim years, I remembered this one scene as something that once occurred, long ago, to my very self, in my own experience. Then came a vast gulf, an unbridged abyss: and after that, with a vividness as of yesterday, the murder.

I held my ears and crouched low, sitting up in my bed in the dark. But the dream seemed to go on still: it remained with me distinctly.

The more I thought it over, the more certain it appeared as part of my own experience. Putting two and two together, I made sure in my own mind this was a genuine recollection of my life in Australia. I was born there, I knew: that I had learned from everybody. But I could distinctly remember having LIVED there now. It came back to me as memory. The dream had reinstated it.

And it was the sight of the photograph that had produced the dream. This was curious, very. A weird idea came across me. Had I begun, in all past efforts to remember, at the wrong end? Instead of trying to recollect the circumstances that immediately preceded the murder, ought I to have set out by trying to reinstate my First Life, chapter by chapter and verse by verse, from childhood upward? Ought I to start by recalling as far as possible my very earliest recollections in my previous existence, and then gradually work up through all my subsequent history to the date of the murder?

The more I thought of it, the more convinced was I that that was the right procedure.

It was certainly significant that this vague childish recollection of something which might have happened when I was just about two years old should be the very first thing to recur to my my memory. Yet so appalled and alarmed was I by the weirdness of this sudden apparition, looming up, as it were, all by itself in the depths of my consciousness, that I hardly dared bring myself to think of trying to recall any other scenes of that dead and past existence. The picture rose like an exhalation, hanging unrelated in mid-air, a mere mental mirage: and it terrified me so much, that I shrank unutterably from the effort of calling up another of like sort to follow it.

CHAPTER IX.

HATEFUL SUSPICIONS

The rest of that night I lay awake in my bed, the scene in the verandah by the big blue-gum-trees haunting me all the time, much as in earlier days the Picture of the murder had pursued and haunted me. Early in the morning I rose up, and went down to Jane in her little parlour. I longed for society in my awe. I needed human presence. I couldn't bear to be left alone by myself with all these pressing and encompassing mysteries.

"Jane," I said after a few minutes' careless talk - for I didn't like to tell her about my wonderful dream, - "where exactly did you find the picture of that house hanging over in the corner there?"

"Lor' bless your heart, miss," Jane answered, "there's a whole boxful of them at The Grange. Nobody ever cared for them. They're up in the top attic. They were locked till your papa died, and then they were opened by order of the executors. Some of 'em's faded even worse than that one, and none of 'em's very good; but I picked this one out because it was better worth framing for my room than most of 'em. The executors took no notice when they found what they was. They opened the box to see if it was dockyments."

"Well, Jane," I said, "I shall go up and bring them every one away with me. It's possible they may help me to recollect things a bit." I drew my hand across my forehead. "It all seems so hazy," I went on. "Yet when I see things again, I sometimes feel as if I almost recognised them."

So that very morning we went up together (I wouldn't go alone), and got the rest of the photographs - very faded positives from old-fashioned plates, most of them representing persons and places I had never seen; and a few of them apparently not taken in England.

I didn't look them all over at once just then. I thought it best not to do so. I would give my memory every possible chance. Take a few at a time, and see what effect they produced on me. Perhaps - though I shrank from the bare idea with horror - they might rouse in my sleep such another stray effort of spontaneous reconstruction. Yet the last one had cost me much nervous wear and tear - much mental agony.

A few days after, I went away from Woodbury. I had learned for the moment, I thought, all that Woodbury could teach me: and I longed to get free again for a while from this pervading atmosphere of mystery. At Aunt Emma's, at least, all was plain and aboveboard. I would go back to Barton-on-the-Sea, and rest there for a while, among the heathery hills, before proceeding any further on my voyage of discovery.

But I took back Jane with me. I was fond of Jane now. In those two short weeks I had learned to cling to her. Though I remembered her, strictly speaking, no more than at first, yet the affection I must have borne her in my First State seemed to revive in me very easily, like all other emotions. I was as much at home with Jane, indeed, as if I had known her for years. And this wasn't strange; for I HAD known her for years, in point of fact; and and though I'd forgotton most of those years, the sense of familiarity they had inspired still lived on with me unconsciously. I know now that memory resides chiefly in the brain, while the emotions are a wider endowment of the nervous system in general; so that while a great shock may obliterate whole tracts in the memory, no power on earth can ever alter altogether the sentiments and feelings.

As for Jane, she was only too glad to come with me. There were no lodgers at present, she said; and none expected. Her sister Elizabeth would take care of the rooms, and if any stranger came, why, Lizzie'd telegraph down at once for her. So I wrote to Aunt Emma to expect us both next day. Aunt Emma's, I knew, was a home where I or mine were always welcome.

Jane had never seen Aunt Emma. There had been feud between the families while my father lived, so she didn't visit The Grange after my mother's death. Aunt Emma had often explained to me in part how all that happened. It was the one point in our family history on which she'd ever been explicit: for she had a grievance there; and what woman on earth can ever suppress her grievances? It's our feminine way to air them before the world, as it's a man's to bury them deep in his own breast and brood over them.

My mother, she told me, had been a widow when my father married her - a rich young widow. She had gone away, a mere girl, to Australia with her first husband, a clergyman, who was lost at sea two or three years after, on the voyage home to England without her. She had one little girl by her first husband, but the child died quite young: and then she married my father, who met her first in Australia while she waited for news of the clergyman's safety. Her family always disapproved of the second marriage. My father had no money, it seemed; and mamma was well off, having means of her own to start with, like Aunt Emma, and having inherited also her first husband's property, which was very considerable. He had left it to his little girl, and after her to his wife; so that first my father, and then I myself, came in, in the end, to both the little estates, though my mother's had been settled on the children of the first marriage. Aunt Emma always thought my father had married for money: and she said he had been hard and unkind to mamma: not indeed cruel; he wasn't a cruel man; but severe and wilful. He made her do exactly as he wished about everything, in a masterful sort of way, that no woman could stand against. He crushed her spirit entirely, Aunt Emma told me; she had no will of her own, poor thing: his individuality was so strong, that it overrode my mother's weak nature rough-shod.

Not that he was rough. He never scolded her; he never illtreated her; but he said to her plainly, "You are to do so and so;" and she obeyed like a child. She never dared to question him.

So Aunt Emma had always said my mother was badly used, especially in money matters - the money being all, when one came to think of it, her own or her first husband's; - and as a consequence, auntie was never invited to The Grange during my father's lifetime.

When we reached Barton-on-the-Sea, Jane and I, on

our way from Woodbury, Aunt Emma was waiting at the station to meet us. To my great disappointment, I could see at first sight she didn't care for Jane: and I could also see at first sight Jane didn't care for her. This was a serious blow to me, for I leaned upon those two more than I leaned upon anyone; and I had far too few friends in the world of my own, to afford to do without any one of them.

In the evening, however, when I went up to my own room to bed, Jane came up to help me as she always did at Woodbury. I began at once to tax her with not liking Aunt Emma. With a little hesitation, Jane admitted that at first sight she hadn't felt by any means disposed to care for her. I pressed her hard as to why. Jane held off and prevaricated. That roused my curiosity: - you see, I'm a woman. I insisted upon knowing.

"Oh, miss, I can't tell you!" Jane cried, growing red in the face, "I can't bear to say it out. You oughtn't to ask. It'll hurt you to know I even thought such a thing of her!"

"You MUST tell me, Jane," I exclaimed, with a cold shudder of terror, half guessing what she meant. "Don't keep me in suspense. Let me know what it is. I'm accustomed to shocks now. I know I can stand them."

Jane answered nothing directly. She only held out her coarse red hand and asked me, with a face growing pale as she spoke:

"Where's that picture of the murder?"

I produced it from my box, trembling inwardly all over.

Jane darted one finger demonstratively at a point in the photograph.

"Whose hand is THAT?" she asked with a strange earnestness, putting her nail on the murderer's.

The words escaped me in a cry of horror almost before I was aware of them:

"Aunt Emma's!" I said, gasping. "I NEVER noticed it before."

Then I drew back and stared at it in speechless awe and consternation.

It was quite, quite true. No use in denying it. The figure that escaped through the window was dressed in man's clothes, to be sure, and as far as one could judge from the foreshortening and the peculiar stoop, had a man's form and stature. But the hand was a woman's - soft, and white, and delicate: nay more, the hand, as I said in my haste, was line for line Aunt Emma's.

In a moment a terrible sinking came over me from head to foot. I trembled like an aspen-leaf. Could this, then, be the meaning of Dr. Marten's warning, that I should let sleeping dogs lie, lest I should be compelled to punish someone whom I loved most dearly? Had Fate been so cruel to me, that I had learned to cling most in my Second State to the very criminal whose act had blotted out my First? Had I grown to treat like a mother my father's murderer?

Aunt Emma's hand! Aunt Emma's hand! That was Aunt Emma's hand, every touch and every line of it. But no! where were the marks, those well-known marks on the palm? I took up the big magnifying-glass with which I had often scanned that photograph close before. Not a sign or a trace of them. I shut my eyes, and called up again the mental Picture of the murder. I looked hard at the phantom-hand in it, that floated like a vision, all distinct before my mind's eye. It was flat and smooth and white. Not a scar - not a sign on it. I turned round to Jane, that too natural detective.

"No, no!" I cried hastily, with a quick tone of triumph. "Aunt Emma's hand is marked on the palm with great gashes and cuts. This one's smooth as smooth can be. And so's the one I can see in the Picture within me!"

Jane drew back with a startled air, and opened her mouth, all agog, to let in a deep breath.

"The wall!" she said slowly. "The bottle-glass, don't you know! The blood on the top! Whoever did it, climbed over and tore his hands. Or HER hands, if it was a woman! That would account for the gashes."

This was more than I could endure. The coincidence was too crushing. I bent down my head on my arms and cried silently, bitterly. I hated Jane in my heart for even suggesting it. Yet I couldn't deny to myself for a moment the strength and suggestiveness of her half-spoken argument.

Not that for a second I believed it true. I could never believe it. Aunt Emma, so gentle, so kindly, so sweet: incapable of hurting any living thing: the tenderest old lady that breathed upon earth: and my own mother's sister, whom I loved as I never before loved anyone! Aunt Emma the murderess! The bare idea was preposterous! I couldn't entertain it. My whole nature revolted from it.

And indeed, how very slight, after all, was the mere scrap of evidence on which Jane ventured to suggest so terrible a charge! A man - in man's clothes - fairly tall and slim, and apparently dark-haired, but stooping so much that he looked almost hump-backed: how different from Aunt Emma, with her womanly figure, and her upright gait, and her sweet old white head! Why, it was clearly ridiculous.

And yet, the fact remained that as Jane pointed to the Picture and asked, "Whose hand is that?" the answer came up all spontaneously to my lips, without hesitation, "Aunt Emma's!"

I sat there long in my misery, thinking it over to myself. I didn't know what to do. I couldn't go and confide to Aunt Emma's ear this new and horrible doubt, - which was no doubt after all, for I KNEW it was impossible. I hated Jane for suggesting it; I hated her for telling me. Yet I couldn't be left alone. I was far too terrified.

"Oh, Jane;" I cried, looking up to her, and yet despising myself for saying it, "you must stop here to-night and sleep with me. If I'm left by myself in the room alone, I know I shall go mad - I can feel it - I'm sure of it!"

Jane stopped with me and soothed me. She was certainly very kind. Yet I felt in a dim underhand sort of way it was treason to Aunt Emma to receive her caresses at all after what she had said to me. Though to be sure, it was I, not she, who spoke those hateful words. It was I myself who had said the hand was Aunt Emma's.

As I lay awake and thought, the idea flashed across me suddenly, could Jane have any grudge of her own against Aunt Emma? Was this a deliberate plot? What did she mean by her warnings that I should keep my mind open? Why had she said from the very first it was a woman's hand? Did she want to set me against my aunt? And was Dr. Marten in league with her? In my tortured frame of mind, I felt all alone in the world. I covered my head and sobbed in my misery. I didn't know who were my friends and who were against me.

At last, after long watching, I dozed off into an uneasy sleep. Jane had already been snoring long beside me. I woke up again with a start. I was cold and shuddering. I had dreamed once more the same Australian dream. My mamma as before stood gentle beside me. She stooped down and smoothed my hair: I could see her face and her form distinctly. And I noticed now she was like her sister, Aunt Emma, only younger and prettier, and ever so much slighter. And her hand, too, was soft and white like auntie's - very gentle and delicate.

It was just there that I woke up - with the hand before my eyes. Oh, how vividly I noted it! Aunt Emma's hand, only younger, and unscarred on the palm. The family hand, no doubt: the hand of the Moores. I remembered, now, that Aunt Emma had spoken more than once of that family peculiarity. It ran through the house, she said. But my hand was quite different: not the Moore type at all: I supposed I must have taken it, as was natural, from the Callinghams.

And then, in my utter horror and loneliness, a still more awful and ghastly thought presented itself to me. This was my mother's hand I saw in the picture. Was it my mother, indeed, who wrought the murder? Was she living or dead? Had my father put upon her some grievous wrong? Had he pretended to get her out of the way? Had he buried her alive, so to speak, in some prison or madhouse? Had she returned in disguise from the asylum or the living grave to avenge herself and murder him? In my present frame of mind, no idea was too wild or too strange for me to entertain. If this strain continued much longer, I should go mad myself with suspense and horror!

CHAPTER X.

YET ANOTHER PHOTOGRAPH

Next morning my head ached. After all I'd suffered, I could hardly bear to recur to the one subject that now always occupied my thoughts. And yet, on the other hand, I couldn't succeed in banishing it. To relieve my mind a little, I took out the photographs I had brought from the box at The Grange, and began to sort them over according to probable date and subject.

They were of different periods, some old, some newer. I put them together in series, as well as I could, by the nature of the surroundings. The most recent of all were my father's early attempts at instantaneous electric photography - the attempts which led up at last to his automatic machine, the acmegraph, that produced all unconsciously the picture of the murder. Some of these comparatively recent proofs represented men running and horses trotting: but the best of all, tied together with a bit of tape, clearly belonged to a single set, and must have been taken at the same time at an athletic meeting. There was one of a flat race, viewed from a little in front, with the limbs of the runners in seemingly ridiculous attitudes, so instantaneous and therefore so grotesquely rigid were they. There was another of a high jump, seen from one side at the very moment of clearing the pole, so that the figure poised solid in mid-air as motionless as a statue. And there was a third, equally successful, of a man throwing the hammer, in which the hammer, in the same way, seemed to hang suspended of itself like Mahomet's coffin between earth and heaven.

But the one that attracted my attention the most was a photograph of an obstacle-race, in which the runners had to mount and climb over a wagon placed obtrusively sideways across the course on purpose to baffle them. This picture was taken from a few yards in the rear; and the athletes were seen in it in the most varied attitudes. Some of them were just climbing up one side of the wagon: others had mounted to the top ledge of the body: and one, standing on the further edge, was in the very act of leaping down to the ground in front of him. He was bent double, to spring, with a stoop like a hunchback, and balanced himself with one hand held tightly behind him.

As my eye fell on that figure, a cold thrill ran through me. For a moment I only knew something important had happened. Next instant I realised what the thrill portended. I could only see the man's back, to be sure, but I knew him in a second. I had no doubt as to who it was. This was HIM - the murderer!

Yes, yes! There could be no mistaking that arched round back that had haunted me so long in my waking dreams. I knew him at sight. It was the man I had seen on the night of the murder getting out of the window!

Perhaps I was overwrought. Perhaps my fancy ran away with me. But I didn't doubt for a second. I rose from my seat, and in a tremulous voice called Jane into the room. Without one word I laid both pictures down before her together. Jane glanced first at the one, then turned quickly to the other. A sharp little cry broke from her lips all unbidden. She saw it as fast and as instinctively as I had done.

"That's him!" she exclaimed, aghast, and as pale as a sheet. "That's him, right enough, Miss Una. That's the very same back! That's the very same hand! That's the man! That's the murderer!"

And indeed, this unanimity was sufficiently startling. For nothing could have been more different than the dress in the two cases. In the murder scene, the man seemed to wear a tweed suit and knickerbockers, - he was indistinct, as I said before, against the blurred light of the window: while in the athletic scene, he wore just a thin jersey and running-drawers, cut short at the knee, with his arms and legs bare, and his muscles contracted. Yet for all that, we both knew him for the same man at once. That stooping back was unmistakable; that position of the hand was characteristic and unique. We were sure he was the same man. I trembled with agitation. I had a clue to the murderer!

Yet, strange to say, that wasn't the first thought that occurred to my mind. In the relief of the moment, I looked up into Jane's eyes, and exclaimed with a sigh of profound relief:

"Then you see how mistaken you were about the hands and Aunt Emma!"

Jane looked close at the hand in the photograph once more.

"Well, it's curious," she said, slowly. "That's a man,

sure enough: but he'd ought to be a Moore. The palm's your aunt's as clear as ever you could paint it!"

I glanced over her shoulder. She was perfectly right. It was a man beyond all doubt, the figure on the wagon. Yet the hand was Aunt Emma's, every line and every stroke of it; except, of course, the scars. Those, I saw at a glance, were wholly wanting.

And now I had really a clue to the murderer.

Yet how slight a clue! Just a photograph of men's backs. What men? When and where? It was an athletic meeting. Of what club or society? That was the next question now I had to answer. Instinctively I made up my mind to answer it myself, without giving any notice to the police of my discovery.

Perhaps I should never have been able to answer it at all but for one of the photographs which, as I thought, though lying loose by itself, formed part of the same series. It represented the end of a hundred-yard race, with the winners coming in at the tape by a pavilion with a flag-staff. On the staff a big flag was flying loosely in the wind. The folds hid half of the words on its centre from sight. But this much at least I could read:

"ER...OM..OY...LETI...UB."

I gazed at them long and earnestly. After a minute or two of thought, I made out the last two words. The inscription must surely be Something-or-other Athletic Club.

But what was "Er... om.. oy..."? That question

staggered me. Gazing harder at it than ever, I could come to no conclusion. It was the name of a place, no doubt: but what place, I knew not.

"Er"? No, "Ber": just a suspicion of a B came round the corner of a fold. If B was the first letter, I might possibly identify it.

I took the photograph down to Aunt Emma, without telling her what I meant. She couldn't bear to think I was ever engaged in thinking of my First State at all.

"Can you read the inscription on that flag, auntie?" I asked. "It's an old photograph I picked up in the attic at The Grange, and I'd like to know, if I could, at what place it was taken."

Aunt Emma gazed at it long and earnestly. Her colour never changed. Then she shook her head quietly.

"I don't know the place," she said; "and I don't know the name. I can't quite make it out. That's E, and R, and O. You see, the letters in between might be almost anything."

I wasn't going to be put off, however, with the port thus in sight. One fact was almost certain. Wherever that pavilion might be, the murderer was there on the day unknown when those photo-graphs were taken. And whatever that day might be, my father and the murderer were there together. That brought the two into connection, and brought me one step nearer a solution than ever the police had been; for hitherto no one had even pretended to have the slightest clue to the personality of the man who jumped out of the window.

I went into the library and took down the big atlas. Opening the map of England and Wales, I began a hopeless search, county by county, from Northumberland downward, for any town or village that would fit these mysterious letters. It was a wild and foolish idea. In the first place not a quarter of the villages were marked in the map; and in the second place, my brain soon got muddled and dazed with trying to fit in the names with the letters on the flag. Two hours had passed away, and I'd only got as far down as Lancashire and Durham. And, most probably even so, I would never come upon it.

Then suddenly, a bright idea broke on my brain at once. The Index! The Index! Presumably, as no fold seemed to obscure the first words, the name began with what looked like a B. That was always something.

A man would have thought of that at once, of course: but then, I have the misfortune to be only a woman.

I turned to the Index in haste, and looked down it with hurried eyes. Almost sooner than I could have hoped, the riddle unread itself. "Ber-, Berb-, Berc-, Berd-," I read out: "Berkshire: Berham: Berhampore: that won't do: Berlin: Berling: Bernina: Berry - what's that? Oh, great heavens!" - my brain reeled - "Berry Pomeroy!"

It was as clear as day. How could I have missed it before? There it seemed to stand out almost legible on the flagstaff. I read it now with ease: "Berry Pomeroy Athletic Club."

I looked up the map once more, following the lines with my fingers, till I found the very place where the name was printed. A village in Devonshire, not far from Torquay. Yes! That's it; Berry Pomeroy. The murderer was there on the day of that athletic meeting!

My heart came up into my mouth with mingled horror and triumph. I felt like a bloodhound who gets on the trail of his man. I would track him down now, no doubt - my father's murderer!

I had no resentment against him, no desire for vengeance. But I had a burning wish to free myself from this environing mystery.

I wouldn't tell the police or the inspector, however, what clue I had obtained. I'd find it all out for myself without anyone's help. I remembered what Dr. Marten had said, and determined to be wise. I'd work on my own lines till all was found out: and then, be it who it might, I sternly resolved I'd let justice be done on him.

So I said nothing even to Jane about the discovery I'd just made. I said nothing to anybody till we sat down at dinner. Then, in the course of conversation, I got on the subject of Devonshire.

"Auntie," I ventured to ask at last, in a very casual way, "did I ever, so far as you know, go anywhere near a place called Berry Pomeroy?"

Aunt Emma gave a start.

"Oh, darling, why do you ask?" she cried.

"You don't mean to say you remember that, do you? What do you want to know for, Una? You can't possibly recollect your Torquay visit, surely!"

I trembled all over. Then I was on the right track!

"Was I ever at Torquay?" I asked once more, as firmly as I could. "And when I was there, did I go over one day to Berry Pomeroy?"

Aunt Emma grew all at once as white as death.

"This is wonderful!" she cried in an agitated voice. "This is wonderful - wonderful! If you can remember that, my child, you can remember anything."

"I DON'T remember it auntie," I answered, not liking to deceive her. "To tell you the truth, I simply guessed at it. But when and why was I at Torquay? Please tell me. And did I go to Berry Pomeroy?" For I stuck to my point, and meant to get it out of her.

Aunt Emma gazed at me fixedly.

"You went to Torquay, dear," she said in a very slow voice, "in the spring of the same year your poor father was killed: that's more than four years ago. The Willie Moores live at Torquay, and several more of your cousins. You went to stop with Willie's wife, and you stayed five weeks. I don't know whether you ever went over to Berry Pomeroy. You may have, and you mayn't: it's within an easy driving distance. Minnie Moore has often written to ask me whether you could go there again; Minnie was always fond of you, and thinks you'd remember her: but I've been afraid to allow you, for fear it should recall sad scenes. She's about your own age, Minnie is; and she's a daughter of Willie Moore, who's my own first cousin, and of course your dear mother's."

I never hesitated a moment. I was strung up too tightly by that time.

"Auntie dear," I said quietly, "I go to-morrow to Torquay. I must know all now. I must hunt up these people."

Auntie knew from my tone it was no use trying to stand in my way any longer.

"Very well, dear," she said resignedly. "I don't believe it's good for you: but you must do as you like. You have your father's will, Una. You were always headstrong."

CHAPTER XI.

THE VISION RECURS

I hated asking auntie questions, they seemed to worry and distress her so; but that evening, in view of my projected visit o Torquay, I was obliged to cross-examine her rather closely about many things. I wanted to know about my Torquay relations, and as far as possible about my mother's family. In the end I learned that the Willie Moores were cousins of ours on my mother's side who had never quarrelled with my father, like Aunt Emma, and through whom alone accordingly, in the days of my First State, Aunt Emma was able to learn anything about me. They had a house at Torquay, and connections all around; for the Moores were Devonshire people. Aunt Emma was very anxious, if I went down there at all, I should stop with Mrs. Moore: for Minnie would be so grieved, she said, if I went to an hotel or took private lodgings. But I wouldn't hear of that myself. I knew nothing of the Moores - in my present condition - and I didn't like to trust myself in the hands of those who to me were perfect strangers. So I decided on going to the Imperial Hotel, and calling on the Moores quietly to pursue my investigation.

Another question I asked in the course of the evening. I had wondered about it often, and now, in these last straits, curiosity overcame me.

"Aunt Emma," I said unexpectedly after a pause, without one word of introduction, "how ever did you get those scars on your hand? You've never told me."

In a moment, Aunt Emma blushed suddenly crimson like a girl of eighteen.

"Una," she answered very gravely, in a low strange tone, "oh, don't ask me about that, dear. Don't ask me about that. You could never understand it.... I got them... in climbing over a high stone wall... a high stone wall, with bits of glass stuck on top of it."

In spite of her prohibition, I couldn't help asking one virtual question more. I gave a start of horror:

"Not the wall at The Grange!" I cried. "Oh, Aunt Emma, how wonderful!"

She gazed at me, astonished.

"Yes, the wall at The Grange," she said simply. "But I don't know how you guessed it.... Oh, Una, don't talk to me any more about these things, I implore you. You can't think how they grieve me. They distress me unspeakably."

Much as I longed to know, I couldn't ask her again after that. She was trembling like an aspen-leaf. For some minutes we sat and looked at the fireplace in silence.

Then curiosity overcame me again.

"Only one question more, auntie," I said. "When I came to you first, you were at home here at Barton. You didn't come to Woodbury to fetch me after the murder. You didn't attend the inquest. I've often wondered at that. Why didn't you bring me yourself? Why didn't you hurry to nurse me as soon as you heard they'd shot my father?"

Aunt Emma gazed at me again with a face like a sheet.

"Darling," she said, quivering, "I was ill. I was in bed. I was obliged to stay away. I'd hurt myself badly a little before.... Oh, Una, leave off! If you go on like this, you'll drive me mad. Say no more, I implore of you."

I couldn't think what this meant; but as auntie wished it, I held my peace, all inwardly trembling with suppressed excitement.

That night, when I went up to bed, I lay awake long, thinking to myself of the Australian scene. In the silence of the night it came back to me vividly. Rain pattered on the roof, and helped me to remember it. I could see the blue-gum trees waving their long ribbon-like leaves in the wind: I could see the cottage, the verandah, my mother, our dog: nay, even, I remembered now, with a burst of recollection, his name was Carlo. The effort was more truly a recollection than before: it was part of myself: I felt aware it was really I myself, not another, who had seen all this, and lived and moved in it.

Slowly I fell asleep, and passed from thinking to dreaming. My dream was but a prolongation of the thoughts I had been turning over in my waking mind. I was still in Australia; still on the verandah of our wooden house; and my mamma was there, and papa beside her. I knew it was papa; for I held his hand and played with him. But he was so much altered, so grave and severe; though he smiled at me good-humouredly. Mamma was sitting behind, with baby on her lap. It seemed to me quite natural she should be there with baby. The scene was so distinct - very vivid and clear. It persisted for many minutes, perhaps even hours. It burnt itself into my brain. At last, it woke me up by its very intensity.

As I woke, a great many thoughts crowded in upon me all at once. This time I knew instantly it was no mere dream, but a true recollection. Yet what a strange recollection! how unexpeted! how incomprehensible! How much in it to settle! how much to investigate and hunt up and inquire about!

In the first place, though I was still in my dream a little girl, much time must have elapsed since the earlier vision; for my papa looked far older, and graver, and sterner. He had more hair about his face, too, a long brown beard and heavy moustache; and when I gazed hard at him mentally, I could recognise the likeness with the white-bearded man who lay dead on the floor: while in my former recollection, I could scarcely make out any resemblance of the features. This showed that the second scene came long after the first: my father must by that time have begun to resemble his later self. A weird feeling stole over me. Was I going to relive my previous life, piecemeal? Was the past going to unroll itself in slow but regular panorama to my sleeping vision? Was my First State to become known like this in successive scenes to my Second?

But that wasn't all. There were strange questions to decide, too, about this new dream of dead days. What could be the meaning of that mysterious baby? She seemed to be so vivid, so natural, so real; her presence there was so much a pure matter of course to me, that I couldn't for a moment separate her from the rest of the Picture. I REMEMBERED the baby, now; as I remembered my mother, and my father, and Australia. There was no room for doubt as to that. The baby was an integral part of my real recollection. Floating across the dim ocean of years, I was certain that night I had once lived in such a scene, with my mamma, and baby.

Yet oh, what baby? I never had a brother or sister of my own, except the half-sister that died - the clergyman's child, Mary Wharton. And Mary, from what I had learned from Aunt Emma and others, must have died when I was only just five months old, immediately before we left Australia. How, then, could I remember her, even in this exalted mental state of trance or dream? And, above all, how could I remember a far earlier scene, when my papa was younger, when his face was smooth, and when there was no other baby?

This mystery only heightened the other mysteries which surrounded my life. I was surfeited with them now. In very despair and listlessness, I turned round on my side, and dozed dreamily off again, unable to grapple with it.

But still that scene haunted me. And still, even in sleep, I asked myself over and over again, "How on earth can this be? What's the meaning of the baby?"

Perhaps it was a little sister that died young, whom I

never had heard of. And perhaps not. In a life such as mine, new surprises are always possible.

Grant Allen

CHAPTER XII.

THE MOORES OF TORQUAY

Strange to say, in spite of everything, my sleep refreshed me. I woke up in the morning strong and vigorous - thank goodness, I have physically a magnificent constitution - and packed my box, with Jane's help, for my Torquay expedition.

I went up to London and down to Torquay alone, though Jane offered to accompany me. I was learning to be self-reliant. It suited my plans better. Nobody could bear this burden for me but myself; and the sooner I learnt to bear it my own way, the happier for me.

At Torquay station, to my great surprise, a fresh-looking girl of my own age rushed up to me suddenly, and kissed me without one word of warning. She was a very pretty girl, pink-cheeked and hazel-eyed: and as she kissed me, she seized both my hands in hers, and cried out to me frankly:

"Why, there you are, Una dear! Cousin Emma telegraphed us what train you'd arrive by; so I've driven down to meet you. And now, you're coming up with us this very minute in the pony-carriage."

"You're Minnie Moore, I suppose?" I said, gazing at her admiringly. Her sweet, frank smile and apple-blossom cheek somehow inspired me with confidence.

She looked back at me quite distressed. Tears rose at once into her eyes with true Celtic suddenness.

"Oh, Una," she cried, deeply hurt and drawing back into her shell, "don't tell me you don't know me! Why, I'm Minnie! Minnie!"

My heart went out to her at once. I took her hand in mine again.

"Minnie dear," I said softly, quite remorseful for my mistake, "you must remember what has happened to me, and not be angry. I've forgotten everything, even my own past life. I've forgotten that I ever before set eyes upon you. But, my dear, there's one thing I've NOT in a way forgotten; and that is, that I loved you and love you dearly. And I 'll give you a proof of it. When I started, I knew none of you; and I told Aunt Emma I wouldn't go among strangers. The moment I see you, I know you're no stranger, but a very dear cousin. When I've forgotten MYSELF, how can I remember YOU? But I'll go up with you at once. And I'll countermand the room I ordered by telegram at the Imperial."

The tears stood fuller in Minnie's eyes than before. She clasped my hand hard. Her pretty lips trembled.

"Una darling," she said, "we always were friends, and we always shall be. If you love me, that's all. You're a darling. I love you."

I looked at her sweet face, and knew it was true. And oh, I was so glad to have a new friend - an old friend, already! For somehow, as always, while the intellectual recollection had faded, the emotion survived. I felt as if I'd known Minnie Moore for years, though I never remembered to have seen her in my life till that minute.

Well, I remained at the Moores' for a week, and felt quite at home there. They were all very nice, Cousin Willie, and Aunt Emily (she made me call her aunt; she said I'd always done so), and Minnie, and all of them. They were really dear people; and blood, after all, is thicker than water. But I made no haste to push inquiries just at first. I preferred to feel my way. I wanted to find out what they knew, if anything, about Berry Pomeroy.

The first time I ventured to mention the subject to Minnie, she gave a very queer smile - a smile of maidenly badinage.

"Well, you remember THAT, any way," she said, in a teasing little way, looking down at me and laughing. "I thought you'd remember that. I must say you enjoyed yourself wonderfully at Berry Pomeroy!"

"Remember what?" I cried, all eagerness; for I saw she attached some special importance to the recollection. And yet, it was terrible she should jest about the clue to my father's murderer!

Minnie looked arch. When she looked arch, she was charming.

"Why, I never saw you prettier or more engaging in

your life than you were that day," she said evasively, as if trying to pique me. "And you flirted so much, too! And everybody admired you so. Everybody on the grounds... especially one person!"

I looked up at her in surprise. I was in my own room, seated by the dressing-table, late at night, when we'd gone up to bed; and Minnie was beside me, standing up, with her bedroom candle in that pretty white little hand of hers.

"What do you mean?" I exclaimed eagerly. "Was it a dance - or a picnic?"

"Oh, you know very well," Minnie went on teasingly, "though you pretend you forget. HE was there, don't you know. You must remember HIM, if you've forgotten all the rest of your previous life. You say you remember the appropriate emotions. Well, he was an emotion: at least, you thought so. It was an Athletic Club Meeting: and Dr. Ivor was there. He went across on his bicycle."

I gave a start of surprise. Minnie looked down at me half maliciously.

"There, you see," she said archly again, "at Dr. Ivor you change colour. I told you you'd remember him!"

I grew pale with astonishment.

"Minnie dear," I said, holding her hands very tight in my own, "it wasn't that, I assure you. I've forgotten him, utterly. If ever I knew a Dr. Ivor, if ever I flirted with him, as you seem to imply, he's gone clean out of my head. His name stirs no chord – recalls absolutely nothing. But I want to know about that Athletic Meeting. Was my poor father there that day? And did he take a set of photographs?"

Minnie clapped her hands triumphantly.

"I KNEW you remembered!" she cried. "Of course, Cousin Vivian was there. We drove over in a break. You MUST remember that. And he took a whole lot of instantaneous photographs."

My hand trembled violently in my cousin's. I felt I was now on the very eve of a great discovery.

"Minnie," I said, tentatively, "do you think your papa would drive us over some day and - and show us the place again?"

"Of course he would, dear," Minnie answered, with a gentle pressure of my hand. "He'd be only too delighted. Whatever you choose. You know you were always such a favourite of daddy's."

I knew nothing of the sort; but I was glad to learn it. I drew Minnie out a little more about the Athletics and my visit to Berry Pomeroy. She wouldn't tell me much: she was too illusive and indefinite: she never could get the notion out of her head, somehow, that I remembered all about it, and was only pretending to forgetfulness. But I gathered from what she said, that Dr. Ivor and I must have flirted a great deal; or, at least, that he must have paid me a good lot of attention. My father didn't like it, Minnie said; he thought Dr. Ivor wasn't well enough off to marry me. He was a distant cousin of ours, of course - everything was always "of course" with that dear bright Minnie - what, didn't I know that? Oh, yes, his mother was one of the Moores of Barnstaple, cousin Edward's people. His name was Courtenay Moore Ivor, you know - though I knew nothing of the sort. And he was awfully clever. And, oh, so handsome!

"Is he at Berry Pomeroy still?" I asked, trembling, thinking this would be a good person to get information from about the people at the Athletic Sports.

"Oh dear, no," Minnie answered, looking hard at me, curiously. "He was never at Berry Pomeroy. He had a practice at Babbicombe. He's in Canada now, you know. He went over six months after Cousin Vivian's death. I think, dear," - she hesitated, - "he never QUITE got over your entirely forgetting him, even if you forgot your whole past history."

This was a curious romance to me, that Minnie thus sprang on me - a romance of my own past life of which I myself knew nothing.

We sat late talking, and I could see Minnie was very full indeed of Dr. Ivor. Over and over again she recurred to his name, and always as though she thought it might rouse some latent chord in my memory. But nothing came of it. If ever I had cared for Dr. Ivor at all, that feeling had passed away utterly with the rest of my experiences.

When Minnie rose to go, I took her hand once more in mine. As I did so, I started. Something about it seemed strangely familiar. I looked at it close with a keen glance. Why, this was curious! It was Aunt Emma's hand: it was my mother's hand: it was the hand in my mental Picture: it was the hand of the murderer!

Grant Allen

"It's just like auntie's," I said with an effort, seeing Minnie noticed my start.

She looked at it and laughed.

"The Moore hand," she said gaily. "We all have it, except you. It's awfully persistent."

I turned it over in front and examined the palm. At sight of it my brain reeled. This was surely magic! Minnie Moore's hand, too, was scarred over with cuts, exactly like Aunt Emma's!"

"Why, how on earth did you do that?" I cried, thunderstruck at the discovery.

But Minnie only laughed again, a bright girlish laugh.

"Climbing over that beastly wall at The Grange," she said with a merry look. "Oh, what fun we did have! We climbed it together. We were dreadful tomboys in those days, dear, you and I: but you were luckier than I was, and didn't cut yourself with the bottle-glass."

This was too surprising to be passed over unnoticed. When Minnie was gone, I lay awake and pondered about it. Had all the Moores got scars on their hands, I wondered? And how many people, I asked myself, had cut themselves time and again in climbing over that barricaded garden-wall of my father's?

The Moore hand might be hereditary, but not surely the scars. Was the murderer, then, a Moore, and was that the meaning of Dr. Marten's warning?

CHAPTER XIII.

DR. IVOR OF BABBICOMBE

Two days later, Cousin Willie drove us over to Berry Pomeroy. The lion of the place is the castle, of course; but Minnie had told him beforehand I wanted, for reasons of my own, to visit the cricket-field where the sports were held "the year Dr. Ivor won the mile race, you remember." So we went there straight. As soon as we entered, I recognised the field at once, and the pavilion, and the woods, as being precisely the same as those presented in the photograph. But I got no further than that. The captain of the cricket-club was on the ground that day, and I managed to get into conversation with him, and strolled off in the grounds. There I showed him the photograph, and asked if he could identify the man climbing over the wagon: but he said he couldn't recognise him. Somebody or other from Torquay, perhaps; not a regular resident. The figures were so small, and so difficult to make sure about. If I'd leave him the photograph, perhaps - but at that I drew back, for I didn't want anybody, least of all at Torquay, to know what quest I was engaged upon.

We drove back, a merry party enough, in spite of my failure. Minnie was always so jolly, and her mirth was contagious. She talked all the way still of Dr. Ivor, half-teasing me. It was all very well my pretending not to remember, she said; but why did I want to see the cricket-field if it wasn't for that? Poor Courtenay! if only he knew, how delighted he'd be to know he wasn't forgotten! For he really took it to heart, my illness - she always called it my illness, and so I suppose it was. From the day I lost my memory, nothing seemed to go right with him; and he was never content till he went and buried himself somewhere in the wilds of Canada.

That evening again, I sat with Minnie in my room. I was depressed and distressed. I didn't want to cry before Minnie, but I could have cried with good heart for sheer vexation. Of course I couldn't bear to go showing the photograph to all the world, and letting everybody see I'd made myself a sort of amateur detective. They would mistake my motives so. And yet I didn't know how I was ever to find out my man any other way. It was that or nothing. I made up my mind I would ask Cousin Willie.

I took out the photograph, as if unintentionally, when I went to my box, and laid it down with my curling-tongs on the table close by Minnie. Minnie took it up abstractedly and looked at it with an indefinite gaze.

"Why, this is the cricket-field!" she cried, as soon as she collected her senses. "One of your father's experi-ments. The earliest acmegraphs. How splendidly they come out! See, that's Sir Everard at the bottom; and there's little Jack Hillier above; and this on one side's Captain Brooks; and there, in front of all - well, you know HIM anyhow, Una. Now, don't pretend you forget! That's Courtenay Ivor!"

Her finger was on the man who stood poised ready to jump. With an awful recoil, I drew back and suppressed a scream. It was on the tip of my tongue to cry out, "Why, that's my father's murderer!"

But, happily, with a great effort of will I restrained myself. I saw it all at a glance. That, then, was the meaning of Dr. Marten's warning! No wonder, I thought, the shock had disorganised my whole brain. If Minnie was right, I was in love once with that man. And I must have seen my lover murder my father!

For I didn't doubt, from what Minnie said, I had really once loved Dr. Ivor. Horrible and ghastly as it might be to realise it, I didn't doubt it was the truth. I had once loved the very man I was now bent on pursuing as a criminal and a murderer!

"You're sure that's him, Minnie?" I cried, trying to conceal my agitation. "You're sure that's Courtenay Ivor, the man stooping on the wagon-top?"

Minnie looked at me, smiling. She thought I was asking for a very different reason.

"Yes, that's him, right enough, dear," she said. "I could tell him among a thousand. Why, the Moore hand alone would be quite enough to know him by. It's just like my own. We've all of us got it - except yourself. I always said you weren't one of us. You're a regular born Callingham."

I gazed at her fixedly. I could hardly speak.

"Oh, Minnie!" I cried once more, "have you ... have you any photograph of him?"

"No, we haven't, dear," Minnie answered.

"That was a fad of Courtenay's, you know. Wherever he went, he'd never be photographed. He was annoyed that day that your father should have taken him unawares. He hated being 'done,' he said. He's so handsome and so nice, but he's not a bit conceited. And he was such a splendid bicyclist! He rode over and back on his bicycle that day, and then ran in all the races as if it were nothing."

A light burst over me at once. This was circumstantial evidence. The murderer who disappeared as if by magic the moment his crime was committed must have come and gone all unseen, no doubt, on his bicycle. He must have left it under the window till his vile deed was done, and then leapt out upon it in a second and dashed off whence he came like a flash of lightning.

It was a premeditated crime, in that case, not the mere casual result of a sudden quarrel.

I must find out this man now, were it only to relieve my own sense of mystery.

"Minnie," I said once more, screwing up my courage to ask, "where's Dr. Ivor now? I mean - that is to say - in what part of Canada?"

Minnie looked at me and laughed.

"There, I told you so!" she said, merrily. "It's not the least bit of use your pretending you're not in love with him, Una. Why, just look how you tremble! You're as white as a ghost! And then you say you don't care for poor Courtenay! I forget the exact name of the place where he lives, but I've got it in my desk, and I can tell you to-morrow. - Oh, yes; it's Palmyra, on the Canada

Pacific. I suppose you want to write to him. Or perhaps you mean to go out and offer yourself bodily."

It was awful having to bottle up the truth in one's own heart, and to laugh and jest like this; but I endured it somehow.

"No, it's not that," I said gravely. "I've other reasons of my own for asking his address, Minnie. I want to go out there, it's true; but not because I cherish the faintest pleasing recollection of Dr. Ivor in any way."

Minnie scanned me over in surprise.

"Well, how you ARE altered, Una!" she cried. "I love you, dear, and like you every bit as much as ever. But you've changed so much. I don't think you're at all what you used to be. You're so grave and sombre."

"No wonder, Minnie," I exclaimed, bursting gladly into tears - the excuse was such a relief - "no wonder, when you think how much I've passed through!"

Minnie flung her arms around my neck, and kissed me over and over again.

"Oh, dear!" she cried, melting. "What have I done? What have I said? I ought never to have spoken so. It was cruel of me - cruel, Una dear. I shall stop here to-night, and sleep with you."

"Oh, thank you, darling!" I cried. "Minnie, that IS good of you. I'm so awfully glad. For to-morrow I must be thinking of getting ready for Canada."

"Canada!" Minnie exclaimed, alarmed. "You're not

really going to Canada! Oh, Una, you're joking! You don't mean to say you're going out there to find him!"

I took her hand in mine, and held it up in the air above her head solemnly.

"Dear cousin," I said, "I love you. But you must promise me this one thing. Whatever may happen, give me your sacred word of honour you'll never tell anybody what we've said here to-night. You'll kill me if you do. I don't want any living soul on earth to know of it."

I spoke so seriously, Minnie felt it was important.

"I promise you," she answered, growing suddenly far graver than her wont. "Oh, Una, I haven't the faintest idea what you mean, but no torture on earth shall ever wring a word of it from me!"

So I went to bed in her arms, and cried myself to sleep, thinking with my latest breath, in a tremor of horror, that I'd found it at last. Courtenay Ivor was the name of my father's murderer!

CHAPTER XIV.

MY WELCOME TO CANADA

The voyage across the Atlantic was long and uneventful. No whales, no icebergs, no excitement of any sort. My fellow-passengers said it was as dull as it was calm. But as for me, I had plenty to occupy my mind meanwhile. Strange things had happened in the interval, and were happening to me on the way. Strange things, in part, of my own internal history.

For before I left England, as I sat with Aunt Emma in her little drawing-room at Barton-on-the-Sea, discussing my plans and devising routes westward, she made me, quite suddenly, an unexpected confession.

"Una," she said, after a long pause, "you haven't told me, my dear, why you're going to Canada. And I don't want to ask you. I know pretty well. We needn't touch upon that. You're going to hunt up some supposed clue to the murderer."

"Perhaps so, Auntie," I said oracularly: "and perhaps not."

For I didn't want it to get talked about and be put into all the newspapers. And I knew now if I wanted to keep it out, I must first be silent.

Aunt Emma drew nearer and took my hand in hers. At the same time, she held up the other scarred and lacerated palm.

"Do you know when I got that, Una?" she asked with a sudden burst. "Well, I'll tell you, my child.... It was the night of your father's death. And I got it climbing over the wall at The Grange, to escape detection."

My blood ran cold once more. What on earth could this mean? Had Auntie - ? But no. I had the evidence of my own senses that it was Courtenay Ivor. I'd tracked him down now. There was no room for doubt. The man on the wagon was the man who fired the shot. I could have sworn to that bent back, of my own knowledge, among a thousand.

I hadn't long to wait, however. Auntie went on after a short pause.

"I was there," she said, "by accident, trying for once to see you."

I looked at her fixedly still, and still I said nothing.

"I was stopping with friends at the time, ten miles off from Woodbury," Aunt Emma went on, smoothing my hand with hers, "and I longed so to see you. I came over by train that day, and stopped late about the town in hopes I might meet you in the street. But I was disappointed. Towards evening I ventured even to go into the grounds of The Grange, and look about everywhere on the chance that I might see you. Perhaps your father might be out. I went round towards the window, which I now know to be the library. As I went, I saw a bicycle leaning up against the wall by the window. I thought that must be some visitor, but still I went on. But just as I reached the window, I saw a flash of electric light; and by the light, I could make out your father's head and beard. He looked as if he were talking angrily and loudly to somebody. The window was open. I was afraid to stop longer. In a sudden access of fear, I ran across the shrubbery towards the garden-wall. To tell you the truth, I was horribly frightened. Why, I don't know; for nothing had happened as yet. I suppose it was just the dusk and the mean sense of intrusion."

She paused and wiped her brow. I sat still, and listened eagerly.

"Presently," she went on, very low, "as I ran and ran, I heard behind me a loud crash - a sound as of a pistol-shot. That terrified me still more. I thought I was being pursued. Perhaps they took me for a burglar. In the agony of my terror, I rushed at the wall in mad haste, and climbed over it anyhow. In climbing, I tore my hand, as you see, and made myself bleed, oh, terribly! However, I persevered, and got down on the other side, with my clothes very little the worse for the scramble. And, fortunately, I was carrying a small light dust-cloak: I put it on at once, and it covered up everything. Then I began to walk along the road as fast as I could in the direction of the station. As I did so, a bicycle shot out from the gate in the opposite direction, going as hard as it could spin, simply flying towards Whittingham. Three minutes later, a man came up to me, breathless. It was the gardener at The Grange, I believe.

"'Have you seen anybody go this way?' he asked. 'A young man, running hard? A young man in knickerbockers?'

"'N - no,' I answered, trembling; for I was afraid to confess. 'Not a soul has gone past!'

"Of course, I didn't know of the murder as yet; and I only wanted to get off unperceived to the station.

"I'd bound up my hand in my handkerchief by that time, and held it tight under my cloak. I went back by train unnoticed, and returned to my friends' house. I hadn't even told them I was going to Woodbury at all. I pretended I'd been spending the day at Whittingham. Next morning, I read in the paper of your father's murder."

I stared hard at Aunt Emma.

"Why didn't you tell me this long ago?" I cried, in an agony of suspense. "Why didn't you give evidence and say so at the inquest?"

"How could I?" Aunt Emma answered, looking back at me appealingly. "The circumstances were too suspicious. As it was, everybody was running after the young man in knickerbockers. Nobody took any notice of a little old lady in a long grey dust-cloak. But if once I'd confessed and shown my wounded hand, who would ever have believed I'd nothing to do with the murder? - except you, perhaps, Una. Oh no: I came back here to my own home as fast as ever I could; for I was really ill. I took to my bed at once. And as nobody called me to give evidence at the inquest, I said nothing to anybody."

"But the bicycle!" I cried. "The bicycle! You ought to

have mentioned that. You were the only one who saw it. It was a clue to the murderer."

"If I'd told," Aunt Emma answered, "I should never have been allowed to take charge of you at all. I thought my one clear duty was to my sister's child: it was to take care of your health in your shattered condition. And even now, Una, I tell you only for this: if you find out anything new, in Canada or here, try not to drag me into it. I couldn't stand the strain. Cross-examination would kill me."

"I'll remember it, auntie," I said, wearied out with excitement. "But I think you did wrong, all the same. In a case like this, it's everybody's first duty to tell all he knows, in the interests of justice."

However, this confession of Aunt Emma's rendered one thing more certain to me than ever before. I was sure I was on the right track now, after Courtenay Ivor. The bicycle clinched the proof.

But I said nothing as yet to the police, or to my friendly Inspector. I was determined to hunt the whole thing up on my own account first, and then deliver my criminal, when fully secured, to the laws of my country.

Not that I was vindictive. Not that I wanted to punish the man. No; I shrank terribly from the task. But to relieve myself from this persistent sense of surrounding mystery, and to free others from suspicion, I felt compelled to discover him. It seemed to me like a duty laid upon me from without. I dared not shirk it.

Grant Allen

On the way out to Quebec, the sea seemed to revive strange memories. I had never crossed it before, except long, long ago, on my way home from Australia. And now that I sat on deck, in a wicker-chair, and looked at the deep dark waves by myself, I began once more, in vague snatches, to recall that earlier voyage. It came back to me all of itself. And that was quite in keeping with my previous recollections. My past life, I felt sure, was unfolding itself slowly to me in regular succession, from childhood onward.

Sitting there on the quarter-deck, gazing hard at the waves, I remembered how I had played on a similar ship years and years before, a little girl in short frocks, with my mamma in a long folding-chair beside me. I could see my mamma, with a sort of frightened smile on her poor pale face; and she looked so unhappy. My papa was there too, somewhat older and greyer - very unlike the papa of my first Australian picture. His face was so much hairier. Mamma cried a good deal at times, and papa tried to comfort her. Besides, what struck me most, there was no more baby. I wasn't even allowed to speak about baby. That subject was tabooed - perhaps because it always made mamma cry so much, and press me hard to her bosom. At any rate, I remembered how once I spoke of baby to some fellow-passenger in the saloon, and papa was very angry, and caught me up in his arms and took me down to my berth; and there I had to stop all day by myself (though it was rolling hard) and could have no fruit for dinner, because I'd been naughty. I was strictly enjoined never to mention baby to anyone again, either then or at any time. I was to forget all about her.

Day after day, as we sailed on, reminiscences of the same sort crowded thicker and thicker upon me. Never reminiscences of my later life, but always early scenes brought up by distinct suggestion of that Australian voyage. When we passed a ship, it burst upon me how we'd passed such ships before: when there was fire-drill on deck, I remembered having assisted years earlier at just such fire-drill. The whole past came back like a dream, so that I could reconstruct now the first five or six years of my life almost entirely. And yet, even so there was a gap, a puzzle, a difficulty somehow. I couldn't make the chronology of this slow-returning memory fit in as it ought with the chronology of the facts given to me by Aunt Emma and the Moores of Torquay. There was a constant discrepancy. It seemed to me that I must be a year or two older at least than they made me out. I remembered the voyage home far too well for my age. I fancied I went back further in my Australian recollections than would be possible from the dates Aunt Emma assigned me.

Slowly, as I compared these mental pictures of my first childhood one with the other, a strange fact seemed to loom forth, incomprehensible, incredible. When first it struck me, all unnerved as I was, my reason staggered before it. But it was true, none the less: quite true, I felt certain. Had I had two papas, then? - for the pictures differed so. Was one, clean-shaven, trim, and in a linen coat, the same as the other, older, graver, and sterner, with much hair on his face, and a rough sort of look, whom I saw more persistently in my later childish memories? I could hardly believe it. One man couldn't alter so greatly in a few short years. Yet I thought of them both alike quite unquestioningly as papa: I thought of them too, I fancied, in a dim sort of way, as one and the same person.

These fresh mysteries occupied my mind for the

greater part of that uneventful voyage. To throw them off, I laughed and talked as much as possible with the rest of the passengers. Indeed, I gained the reputation of being "an awfully jolly girl," so heartily did I throw myself into all the games and amusements, to escape from the burden of my pressing thoughts: and I believe many old ladies on board were thoroughly scandalised that a woman whose father had been brutally murdered should ever be able to seem so bright and lively again. How little they knew! And what a world of mystery seemed to oppress and surround me!

At last, early one morning, we reached the Gulf, and took in our pilot off the Straits of Belleisle. I was on deck at the time, playing a game called "Shovelboard." As the pilot reached the ship, he took the captain's hand, and, to my immense surprise, said in an audible voice:

"So you've the famous Miss Callingham for a passenger, I hear, this voyage. There's the latest Quebec papers. You'll see you're looked for. Our people are expecting her."

I rushed forward, fiery hot, and with a trembling hand took one of the papers he was distributing all round, right and left, to the people on deck. It was unendurable that the memory of that one event should thus dog me through life with such ubiquitous persistence. I tore open the sheet. There, with horrified eyes, I read this hateful paragraph, in the atrociously vulgar style of Transatlantic journalism:

"The Sarmatian, expected off Belleisle to-morrow morning, brings among her passengers, as we learn by telegram, the famous Una Callingham, whose connection with the so-called Woodbury Mystery is now a matter of historical interest. The mysterious two-souled lady possesses, at present, all her faculties intact, as before the murder, and is indeed, people say, a remarkably spry and intelligent young person; but she has most conveniently forgotten all the events of her past life, and more particularly the circumstances of her father's death, which is commonly conjectured to have been due to the pistol of some unknown lover. Such freaks of memory are common, we all know, in the matter of small debts and of newspaper subscriptions, but they seldom extend quite so far as the violent death of a near relation. However, Una knows her own business best. The Sarmatian is due alongside the Bonsecours Quay at 10 a.m. on Wednesday, the 10th; and all Quebec will, no doubt, be assembled at the landing-stage to say 'Good-morning' to the two-souled lady."

The paper dropped from my hand. This was too horrible for anything! How I was ever to go through the ordeal of the landing at Quebec after that, I hadn't the faintest conception. And was I to be dogged and annoyed like this through all my Canadian trip by anonymous scribblers? Had these people no hearts? no consideration for the sensitiveness of an English lady?

I looked over the side of the ship at the dark-blue water. Oh, how I longed to plunge into it and be released for ever from this abiding nightmare!

CHAPTER XV.

A NEW ACQUAINTANCE

The moment we reached the quay at Quebec, some two days later, a dozen young men, with little notebooks in their hands, jumped on board all at once.

"Miss Callingham!" they cried with one accord, making a dash for the quarter-deck. "Which is she? Oh, this! - If you please, Miss Callingham, I should like to have ten minutes of your time to interview you!"

I clapped my hands to my ears, and stood back, all horrified. What I should have done, I don't know, but for a very kind man in a big rough overcoat, who had jumped on board at the same time, and made over to me like the reporters. He stepped up to me at once, pushed aside the young men, and said in a most friendly tone:

"Miss Callingham, I think? You'd better come with me, then. These people are all sharks. Everybody in Quebec's agog to see the Two-souled Lady. Answer no questions at all. Take not the least notice of them. Just follow me to the Custom House. Let them rave, but don't speak to them."

"Who are you?" I asked blindly, clinging to his arm in my terror.

"I'm a policeman in plain clothes," my new friend answered; "and I've been specially detailed by order for this duty. I'm here to look after you. You've friends in Canada, though you may have quite forgotten them. They've sent me to help you. Those are two of my chums there, standing aside by the gangway. We'll walk you off between us. Don't be afraid. - Here, you sir, there; make way! - No one shall come near you."

I was so nervous, and so ashamed that I accepted my strange escort without inquiry or remonstrance. He helped me, with remarkable politeness for a common policeman, across to the Custom House, where I sat waiting for my luggage. Reporters and sightseers, meanwhile, pressed obtrusively around me. My protector held them back. I was half wild with embarrassment. I'm naturally a reserved and somewhat sensitive girl, and this American publicity made me crimson with bashfulness.

As I sat there waiting, however, the two other policemen to whom my champion had beckoned sat one on each side of me, keeping off the idle crowd, while my first friend looked after the luggage and saw it safely through the Customs for me. He must be an Inspector, I fancied, or some other superior officer, the officials were so deferential to him. I gave him my keys, and he looked after everything himself. I had nothing, for my part, to do but to sit and wait patiently for him.

As soon as he had finished, he called a porter to his side.

"Vite!" he cried, in a tone of authority, to the man. "Un fiacre!"

And the porter called one.

I started to find that I knew what he meant. Till that moment, in my Second State, I had learned no French, and didn't know I could speak any. But I recognised the words quite well as soon as he uttered them. My lost knowledge reasserted itself.

They bundled on my boxes. The crowd still stood around and gaped at me, open-mouthed. I got into the cab, more dead than alive.

"Allez!" my policeman cried to the French-Canadian driver, seating himself by my side.

"A la gare du chemin de fer Pacific! Aussi vite que possible!"

I understood every word. This was wonderful. My memory was coming back again.

The man tore along the streets to the Pacific railway station. By the time we reached it we had distanced the sightseers, though some of them gave chase. My policeman got out.

"The train's just going!" he said sharply. "Don't take a ticket for Palmyra, if you don't want to be followed and tracked out all the way. They'll telegraph on your destination. Book to Kingston instead, and then change at Sharbot Lake, and take a second ticket on from there to Palmyra."

I listened, half dazed. Palmyra was the place where Dr. Ivor lived. Yet, even in the hurry of the moment, I wondered much to myself how the policeman knew I wanted to go to Palmyra.

There was no time to ask questions, however, or to deliberate on my plans. I took my ticket as desired, in a turmoil of feelings, and jumped on to the train. I trusted by this time I had eluded detection. I ought to have come, I saw now, under a feigned name. This horrid publicity was more than I could endure. My policeman helped me in with his persistent politeness, and saw my boxes checked as far as Sharbot Lake for me. Then he handed me the checks.

"Go in the Pullman," he said quietly. "It's a long journey, you know: four-and-twenty hours. You've only just caught it. But if you'd stopped in Quebec, you'd never have been able to give the sightseers the slip. You'd have been pestered all through. I think you're safe now. It was this or nothing."

"Oh, thank you so much!" I cried, with heartfelt gratitude, leaning out of the window as the train was on the point of starting. I pulled out my purse, and drew timidly forth a sovereign. "I've only English money," I said, hesitating, for I didn't know whether he'd be offended or not at the offer of a tip - he seemed such a perfect gentleman. "But if that's any use to you - "

He smiled a broad smile and shook his head, much amused.

"Oh, thank you," he said, half laughing, with a very curious air. "I'm a policeman, as I told you. But I don't need tips. I'm the Chief Constable of Quebec - there's my card; Major Tascherel, - and I'm glad to be of use, I'm sure, to any friend of Dr. Ivor's."

He lifted his hat with the inborn grace of a high-born gentleman. I coloured and bowed. The train steamed out of the station. As it went, I fell back, half fainting, in the comfortable armchair of the Pullman car, hardly able to speak with surprise and horror. It was all so strange, so puzzling, so bewildering! Then I owed my escape from the stenographic myrmidons of the Canadian Press to the polite care and attention of my father's murderer!

Major Tascherel was a friend, he said, of Dr. Ivor's!

Then Dr. Ivor knew I had come. He knew I was going to Palmyra to find him. And yet he had written to Quebec, apparently, expecting this crush, and asking his friend the Chief Constable to protect and befriend me. Had he murdered my father, and was he in love with me still? Did he think I'd come out, not to track him down, but to look for him? Strange, horrible questions! My heart stood still within me at this extraordinary revelation. Yet I was so frightened at the moment, alone in a strange land, that I felt almost grateful to the murderer himself for his kindness in thinking of me and providing for my reception.

As I settled in my seat and had time to realise what these things meant, it dawned upon me by degrees that all this was less remarkable, after all, than I first thought it. For they had telegraphed from England that I sailed on the Sarmatian; and Dr. Ivor, like everybody else, must have read the telegram. He might naturally conclude I would be half-mobbed by reporters; and as it was clear he had once been fond of me - hateful as I felt it even to admit the fact to myself - he might really have desired to save me annoyance and trouble. It was degrading, to be sure, even to think I owed anything of any sort to such a wretch as that murderer; yet in a certain corner of my heart I couldn't help being thankful to him. But how strange to feel I had come there on purpose to hunt him down! How horrible that I must so repay good with evil!

Then a still more ghastly thought surged up suddenly in my mind. Why on earth did he think I was going to Palmyra? Was it possible he fancied I loved him still - that I wanted to marry him? Could he imagine I'd come out just to fling myself at his feet and ask him to take me? Could he suppose I'd forgotten all the rest of my past life, and his vile act as well, and yet remembered alone what little love, if any, I ever had borne him? It was incredible that any man, however wicked, however conceited, should think such folly as that - that a girl would marry her father's murderer; and yet what might not one expect from a man who, after having shot my father, had still the inconceivable and unbelievable audacity to take deliberate steps for securing my own comfort and happiness? From such a wretch as that, one might look for almost anything!

For ten minutes or more, as we whirled along the line in the Pullman car, I was too dazed and confused to notice anything around me. My brain swam vaguely, filled full with wild whirling thoughts; the strange drama of my life, always teeming with mysteries, seemed to culminate in this reception in an unknown land by people who appeared almost to know more about my business than I myself did. I gazed out of the window blankly. In some vague dim way I saw we were passing between rocky hills, pine-clad and beautiful, with deep glimpses now and then into the riven gorge of a noble river. But I didn't even realise to myself that these were Canadian hills - those were the heights of Abraham - that was the silver St. Lawrence. It all passed by like a living dream. I sat still in my chair, as one stunned and faint; I gazed out, more dead than alive, on the unfamiliar scene that unrolled itself in exquisite panorama before me. Quebec and the Laurentian hills were to me half unreal: the inner senses alone were awake and conscious.

Presently a gentle voice at my side broke, not at all unpleasantly, the current of my reflections. It was a lady's voice, very sweet and musical.

"I'm afraid," it said kindly, with an air of tender solicitude, "you only just caught the train, and were hurried and worried and flurried at the last at the station. You look so white and tired. How your breath comes and goes! And I think you're new to our Canadian ways. I saw you didn't understand about the checks for the baggage. Let me take away this bag and put it up in the rack for you. Here's a footstool for your feet; that'll make you more comfortable."

At the first sound of her sweet voice, I turned to look at the speaker. She was a girl, perhaps a year or two younger than myself, very slender and graceful, and with eyes like a mother's. She wasn't exactly pretty, but her face was so full of intelligence and expression that it was worth a great deal more than any doll-like prettiness.

Perhaps it was pleasure at being spoken to kindly at all in this land of strangers; perhaps it was revulsion from the agony of shame and modesty I had endured at Quebec; but, at any rate, I felt drawn at first sight to my sweet-voiced fellow-traveller. Besides, she reminded me somewhat of Minnie Moore, and that resemblance alone was enough to attract me. I looked up at her gratefully.

"Oh, thank you so much!" I cried, putting my bag in her hand. "I've only just come out from England; and I'd hardly time at Quebec to catch the train; and the people crowded around so, that I was flustered at landing; and everything somehow seems to be going against me."

And with that my poor overwrought nerves gave way all at once, and without any more ado I just burst out crying.

The lady by my side leant over me tenderly.

"There - cry, dear," she said, as if she'd known me for years, stooping down and almost caressing me. "Jack," - and she turned to a tall gentleman at her side, - "quick! you've got my black bag; get me out the sal volatile. She's quite faint, poor thing; we must look after her instantly."

The person to whom she spoke, and who was apparently her husband or her brother, took down the black bag from the rack hastily, and got out the sal volatile, as my friend directed him. He poured a little into a tumbler and held it quietly to my lips. I liked his manner, as I'd liked the lady's. He was so very brotherly. Besides, there was something extremely soothing about his quick, noiseless way. He did it all so fast, yet without the faintest sign of agitation. I couldn't help thinking what a good nurse he would make; he was so rapid and effective, yet so gentle and so quiet. He seemed perfectly accustomed to the ways of nervous women.

I dried my eyes after a while, and looked up in his face. He was very good-looking, and had a charming soft smile. How lucky I should have tumbled upon such pleasant travelling companions! In my present mental state, I had need of sympathy. And, indeed, they took as much care of me, and coddled me up as tenderly, as if they'd known me for years. I was almost tempted to make a clean breast of my personality to them, and tell them why it was I had been so worried and upset by my reception at Quebec: but I shrank from confessing it. I hated my own name, almost, it seemed to bring me such very unpleasant notoriety.

In a very few minutes, I felt quite at home with my new friends. I explained to them that when I landed I had no intention of going on West by train at once, but that news which I received on the way had compelled me to push forward by the very first chance; and that I had to change my ticket at a place called Sharbot Lake, whose very position or distance I hadn't had time to discover. The lady smiled sweetly, and calmed my fears by telling me we wouldn't reach Sharbot Lake till mid-day to-morrow, and that I would have plenty of time there to book on to my destination.

Thus encouraged, I went on to tell them I had no Canadian money, having brought out what I needed for travelling expenses and hotels in Bank of England 20 pound notes. The lady smiled again, and said in the friendliest way:

"Oh, my brother'll get them changed for you at Montreal as we pass, won't you, Jack? or at least as much as you need till you get to" - she checked herself - "the end of your journey."

I noticed how she pulled herself up, though at the moment I attached no particular importance to it.

So he was her brother, not her husband, then! Well, he was a very nice fellow, either way, and nobody could be kinder or more sympathetic than he'd been to me so far.

We fell into conversation, which soon by degrees grew quite intimate.

"How far West are you going?" the man she called Jack asked after a little time, tentatively.

And I answered, all unsuspiciously:

"To a place called Palmyra."

"Why, we live not far from Palmyra," the sister replied, with a smile. "We're going that way now. Our station's Adolphus Town, the very next village."

I hadn't yet learned to join the wisdom of the serpent to the innocence of the dove, I'm afraid. Remember, though in some ways I was a woman full grown, in others I was little more than a four-year-old baby.

"Do you know a Dr. Ivor there?" I asked eagerly, leaning forward.

"Oh, yes, quite well," the lady answered, arranging my

footstool more comfortably as she spoke. "He's got a farm out there now, and hardly practises at all. How queer it is! One always finds one knows people in common. Is Dr. Ivor a friend of yours?"

I recoiled at the stray question almost as if I'd been shot.

"Oh, no!" I cried, horrified at the bare idea of such treason. "He's anything but a friend... I - I only wanted to know about him."

The lady looked at Jack, and Jack looked at the lady. Were they telegraphing signs? I fancied somehow they gave one another very meaning glances. Jack was the first to speak, breaking an awkward silence.

"You can't expect everyone to know your own friends, or to like them either, Elsie," he said slowly, with his eyes fixed hard on her, as if he expected her to flare up.

My heart misgave me. A hateful idea arose in it. Could my sweet travelling companion be engaged - to my father's murderer?

"But he's a dear good fellow, for all that, Jack," Elsie said stoutly; and strange as it sounds to say so, I admired her for sticking up for her friend Dr. Ivor, if she really liked him. "I won't hear him run down by anybody, not even by YOU. If this lady knew him better, I'm sure she'd like him, as we all do."

Jack turned the conversation abruptly.

"But if you're going to Palmyra," he asked, "where do

you mean to stop? Have you thought about lodgings? You mustn't imagine it's a place like an English town, with an inn or hotel or good private apartments. There's nowhere you can put up at in these brand-new villages. Are you going to friends, or did you expect to find quarters as easily as in England?"

This was a difficulty which, indeed, had never even occurred to me till that moment. I stammered and hesitated.

"Well," I said slowly, "to tell you the truth, I haven't thought about that. The landing at Quebec was such a dreadful surprise to me, and" - tears came into my eyes again - "I had a great shock there - and I had to come on so quick, I didn't ask about anything but catching the train. I meant to stop a night or two either at Quebec or in Montreal, and to make all inquiries: but circumstances, you see, have prevented that. So I really don't know what I'd better do when I get to Palmyra."

"I do," my new friend answered quickly, her soft sweet voice having quite a decisive ring in it. "You'd better not go on to Palmyra at all. There's no sort of accommodation there, except a horrid drinking-saloon. You'd better stop short at Adolphus Town and spend the night with us; and then you can look about you next day, if you like, and see what chance there may be of finding decent quarters. Old Mrs. Wilkins might take her in, Jack, or the Blacks at the tannery."

I smiled, and felt touched.

"Oh, how good of you!" I cried. "But I really couldn't think of it. Thank you ever so much, though, for your kind thought, all the same. It's so good and sweet of you. But you don't even know who I am. I have no introduction."

"You're your own best introduction," Elsie said, with a pretty nod: I thought of her somehow from the very first moment I heard her name as Elsie. "And as to your not knowing us, never mind about that. We know YOU at first sight. It's the Canadian way to entertain Angels unawares. Out here, you know, hospitality's the rule of the country."

Well, I demurred for a long time; I fought off their invitation as well as I could: I couldn't bear thus to quarter myself upon utter strangers. But they both were so pressing, and brought up so many cogent arguments why I couldn't go alone to the one village saloon - a mere whisky-drinking public-house, they said, of very bad character, - that in the long run I was fain almost to acquiesce in their kind plan for my temporary housing. Besides, after my horrid experience at Quebec, it was such a positive relief to me to meet anybody nice and delicate, that I couldn't find it in my heart to refuse these dear people. And then, perhaps it was best not to go quite on to Palmyra at once, for fear of unexpectedly running against my father's murderer. If I met him in the street, and he recognised me and spoke to me, what on earth could I do? My head was all in a whirl, indeed, as to what he might intend or expect: for I felt sure he expected me. I made one last despairing effort.

"If I stop at your house, though," I said, half ashamed of myself for venturing to make conditions, "there's one promise you must make me - that I sha'n't see Dr. Ivor unless you let me know and get my consent beforehand."

Jack, as I called him to myself, answered gaily back with a rather curious smile:

"If you like, you need see nobody but our own two selves. We'll promise not to introduce anybody to you without due leave, and to let you do as you like in that and in everything."

So I yielded at last.

"Well, I must know your name," I said tentatively.

And Jack, looking queerly at me with an inquiring air, said:

"My sister's name's Elsie; mine's John Cheriton."

"And yours?" Elsie asked, glancing timidly down at me.

My heart beat hard. I was face to face with a dilemma. These were friends of Courtenay Ivor's, and I had given myself away to them. I was going to their house, to accept their hospitality - and to betray their friend! Never in my life did I feel so guilty before. Oh! what on earth was I to do? I had told them too much; I had gone to work foolishly. If I said my real name, I should let out my whole secret. I must brazen it out now. With tremulous lips and flushed cheek, I answered quickly, "Julia Marsden."

Elsie drew back, all abashed. In a moment her cheek grew still redder, I felt sure, than my own.

"Oh, Marsden!" she cried, eyeing me close. "Why, I thought you were Miss Callingham!"

"How on earth did you know that?" I exclaimed, terrified almost out of my life. Was I never for one moment to escape my own personality?

"Why, they put it in the papers that you were coming," Elsie answered, looking tenderly at me, more in sympathy than in anger. "And it's written on your bag, you know, that Jack put up in the rack there... That's why we were so sorry for you, and so grieved at the way you must have been hustled on the quay. And that's also why we wanted you to come to us... But don't be a bit afraid. We quite understand you want to travel incognita. After the sort of reception you got at Quebec, no wonder you're afraid of these hateful sightseers!... Very well, dear," she took my hand with the air of an old friend, "your disguise shall be respected while you stop at our house. Miss Marsden let it be. You can make any inquiries you like about Dr. Ivor. We will be secrecy itself. We'll say nothing to anyone. And my brother'll take your ticket at Sharbot Lake for Adolphus Town."

I broke down once more. I fairly cried at such kindness.

"Oh, how good you are!" I said. "How very, very good. This is more than one could ever have expected from strangers."

She held my hand and stroked it.

"We're not strangers," she answered. "We're English ourselves. We sympathise deeply with you in this new, strange country. You must treat us exactly like a brother and sister. We liked you at first sight, and we're sure we'll get on with you."

I lifted her hand to my lips and kissed it.

"And I liked you also," I said, "and your brother, too. You're both so good and kind. How can I ever sufficiently thank you?"

CHAPTER XVI.

MY PLANS ALTER

The rest of that day we spent chatting very amicably in our Pullman arm-chairs. I couldn't understand it myself - when I had a moment to think, I was shocked and horrified at it. I was so terribly at home with them. These were friends of Dr. Ivor's - friends of my father's murderer! I had come out to Canada to track him, to deliver him over, if I could, to the strong hand of Justice. And yet, there I was talking away with his neighbours and friends as if I had known them all my life, and loved them dearly. Nay, what was more, I couldn't in my heart of hearts help liking them. They were really sweet people - so kind and sympathetic, so perceptive of my sensitiveness. They asked no questions that could hurt me in any way. They showed no curiosity about the object of my visit or my relation to Dr. Ivor. They were kindness and courtesy itself. I could see Mr. Cheriton was a gentleman in fibre, and Elsie was as sweet as any woman on earth could be.

By-and-by, the time came for the Pullman saloon to be transformed for the night into a regular sleeping-car. All this was new to me, and I watched it with interest. As soon as the beds were made up, I crept into my berth, and my new friend Elsie took her place on the sofa below me. I lay awake long and thought over the situation. The more I thought of it, the stranger it all seemed. I tried hard to persuade myself I was running some great danger in accepting the Cheritons' invitation. Certainly, I had behaved with consummate imprudence. Canada is a country, I said to myself, where they kidnap and murder well-to-do young Englishmen. How much easier, then, to kidnap and murder a poor weak stray English girl! I was entirely at the mercy of the Cheritons, that was clear: and the Cheritons were Dr. Ivor's friends. As I thought all the circumstances over, the full folly of my own conduct came home to me more and more. I had let these people suppose I was travelling under an assumed name. I had let them know my ticket was not for Palmyra but for Kingston, where I didn't mean to go. I had told them I meant to change it at Sharbot Lake. So they were aware that no one on earth but themselves had any idea where I had gone. And I had further divulged to them the important fact that I had plenty of ready money in Bank of England notes! I stood aghast at my own silliness. But still, I did NOT distrust them.

No, I did NOT distrust them. I felt I ought to be distrustful. I felt it might be expected of me. But they were so gentle-mannered and so sweet-natured, that I couldn't distrust them. I tried very hard, but distrust wouldn't come to me. That kind fellow Jack - I thought of him, just so, as Jack already - couldn't hurt a fly, much less kill a woman. It grieved me to think I would have to hurt his feelings.

For now that I came to look things squarely in the face in my berth by myself, I began to see how utterly impossible it would be for me after all to go and stop with the Cheritons. How I could ever have dreamt it feasible I could hardly conceive. I ought to have refused at once. I ought to have been braver. I ought to have said outright, "I'll have nothing to do or say with anyone who is a friend or an acquaintance of Courtenay Ivor's." And yet, to have said so would have been to give up the game for lost. It would have been to proclaim that I had come out to Canada as Courtenay Ivor's enemy.

I wasn't fit, that was the fact, for my self-imposed task of private detective.

A good part of that night I lay awake in my berth, bitterly reproaching myself for having come on this wild-goose chase without the aid of a man - an experienced officer. Next morning, I rose and breakfasted in the car. The Cheritons breakfasted with me, and, sad to say, seemed more charming than ever. That good fellow Jack was so attentive and kind, I almost felt ashamed to have to refuse his hospitality; and as for Elsie, she couldn't have treated me more nicely or cordially if she'd been my own sister. It wasn't what they said that touched my heart: it was what they didn't say or do - their sweet, generous reticence.

After breakfast, I steeled myself for the task, and broke it to them gently that, thinking it over in the night, I'd come to the conclusion I couldn't consistently accept their proffered welcome.

"I don't know how to say NO to you," I cried, "after you've been so wonderfully kind and nice; but reasons which I can't fully explain just now make me feel it would be wrong of me to think of stopping with you. It would hamper my independence of action to be in anybody else's house. I must shift for myself, and try if

I can't find board and lodging somewhere."

"Find it with us then!" Elsie put in eagerly. "If that's all that's the matter, I'm sure we're not proud - are we, Jack? - not a bit. Sooner than you should go elsewhere and be uncomfortable in your rooms, I'd take you in myself, and board you and look after you. You could pay what you like; and then you'd retain your independence, you see, as much as ever you wanted."

But her brother interrupted her with a somewhat graver air:

"It goes deeper than that, I'm afraid, Elsie," he said, turning his eye full upon her. "If Miss Callingham feels she couldn't be happy in stopping with us, she'd better try elsewhere. Though where on earth we can put her, I haven't just now the very slightest idea. But we'll turn it over in our own minds before we reach Adolphus Town."

There was a sweet reasonableness about Jack that attracted me greatly. I could see he entered vaguely into the real nature of my feelings. But he wouldn't cross-question me: he was too much of a gentleman.

"Miss Callingham knows her own motives best," he said more than once, when Elsie tried to return to the charge. "If she feels she can't come to us, we must be content to do the best we can for her with our neighbours. Perhaps Mrs. Walters would take her in: she's our clergyman's wife, Miss Callingham, and you mightn't feel the same awkwardness with her as with my sister."

"Does she know - Dr. Ivor?" I faltered out, unable to

conceal my real reasons entirely.

"Not so intimately as we do," Jack answered, with a quick glance at his sister. "We might ask her at any rate. There are so few houses in Palmyra or the neighbourhood where you could live as you're accustomed, that we mustn't be particular. But at least you'll spend one night with us, and then we can arrange all the other things afterward."

My mind was made up.

"No, not even one night," I said. I couldn't accept hospitality from Dr. Ivor's friends. Between his faction and mine there could be nothing now but the bitterest enmity. How dare I even parley with people who were friends of my father's murderer?

Yet I was sorry to disappoint that good fellow, Jack, all the same. Did he want me to sleep one night at his house on purpose to rob me and murder me? Girl as I was, and rendered timorous in some ways by the terrible shocks I had received, I couldn't for one moment believe it. I KNEW he was good: I KNEW he was honourable, gentle, a gentleman.

So, journeying on all morning, we reached Sharbot Lake, still with nothing decided. At the little junction station, Jack got me my ticket. That was the turning point in my career. The die was cast. There I lost my identity. A crowd lounged around the platform, and surged about the Pullman car, calling to see "Una Callingham." But no Una Callingham appeared on the scene. I went, on in the same train, without a word to anyone, all unknown save to the two Cheritons, and as an unrecognised unit of common humanity. I had cast that horrid identity clean behind me.

The afternoon was pleasant. In spite of my uncertainty, it gave me a sense of pleased confidence to be in the Cheritons' company. I had taken to them at once: and the more I talked with them, the better I liked them. Especially Jack, that nice brotherly Jack, who seemed almost like an old friend to me. You get to know people so well on a long railway journey. I was quite sorry to think that by five o'clock that afternoon we should reach Adolphus Town, and so part company.

About ten minutes to five, we were collecting our scattered things, and putting our front-hair straight by the mirror in the ladies' compartment.

"Well, Miss Cheriton," I said warmly, longing to kiss her as I spoke, "I shall never forget how kind you two have been to me. I do wish so much I hadn't to leave you like this. But it's quite inevitable. I don't see really how I could ever endure -"

I said no more, for just at that moment, as the words trembled on my lips, a terrible jar thrilled suddenly through the length and breadth of the carriage. Something in front seemed to rush into us with a deep thud. There was a crash, a fierce grating, a dull hiss, a clatter. Broken glass was flying about. The very earth beneath the wheels seemed to give way under us. Next instant, all was blank. I just knew I was lying, bruised and stunned and bleeding, on a bare dry bank, with my limbs aching painfully.

I guessed what it all meant. A collision, no doubt. But I lay faint and ill, and knew nothing for the moment as to what had become of my fellow-passengers.

Grant Allen

CHAPTER XVII.

A STRANGE RECOGNITION

Gradually I was aware of somebody moistening my temples. A soft palm held my hand. Elsie was leaning over me. I opened my eyes with a start.

"Oh, Elsie," I cried, "how kind of you!"

It seemed to me quite natural to call her Elsie.

Even as I spoke, somebody else raised my head and poured something down my throat. I swallowed it with a gulp. Then I opened my eyes again.

"And Jack, too," I murmured.

It seemed as if he'd been "Jack" to me for years and years already.

"She knows us!" Elsie cried, clasping her hands. "She's much better - much better. Quick, Jack, more brandy! And make haste there - a stretcher!"

There was a noise close by. Unseen hands lifted me up, and Jack laid me on the stretcher. Half-an-hour at least must have elapsed, I felt since the first shock of the accident. I had been unconscious meanwhile. The actual crash came and went like lightning. And my memory of all else was blotted out for the moment.

Next, as I lay still, two men took the stretcher and carried me off at a slow pace, under Jack's direction. They walked single-file along the line, and turned down a rough road that led off near a river. I didn't ask where they were going: I was too weak and feeble. At last they came to a house, a small white wooden cottage, very colonial and simple, but neat and pretty. There was a garden in front, full of old-fashioned flowering shrubs; and a verandah ran round the house, about whose posts clambered sweet English creepers.

They carried me in, and laid me down on a bed, in a sweet little room, very plain but dainty. It was panelled with polished pitchpine, and roses peeped in at the open window. Everything about the cottage bore the impress of native good taste. I knew it was Jack's home. It was just such a room as I should have expected from Elsie.

The bed on which they placed me was neat and soft. I lay there dozing with pain. Elsie sat by my side, her own arm in a sling. By-and-by, an Irish maid came in and undressed me carefully under Elsie's direction. Then Elsie said to me, half shrinking:

"Now you must see the doctor."

"Not Dr. Ivor!" I cried, waking up to a full sense of this new threatened horror. "Whatever I do, dear, I WON'T see Dr. Ivor!"

Jack had come in while she spoke, and was standing by the bed, I saw now. The servant had gone out. He lifted my arm, and held my wrist in his hand.

"I'm a doctor myself, Miss Callingham," he said softly, with that quiet, reassuring voice of his. "Don't be alarmed at that; nobody but myself and Elsie need come near you in any way."

I smiled at his words, well pleased.

"Oh, I'm so glad you're a doctor!" I cried, much relieved at the news; "for I'm not the least little bit in the world afraid of YOU. I don't mind your attending me. I like to have you with me." For I had always a great fancy for doctors, somehow.

"That's well," he said, smiling at me such a sweet sympathetic smile as he felt my pulse with his finger. "Confidence is the first great requisite in a patient: it's half the battle. You're not seriously hurt, I hope, but you're very much shaken. Whether you like it or not, you'll have to stop here now for some days at least, till you're thoroughly recovered."

I'm ashamed to write it down; but I was really pleased to hear it. Nothing would have induced me to go voluntarily to their house with the intention of stopping there - for they were friends of Dr. Ivor's. But when you're carried on a stretcher to the nearest convenient house, you're not responsible for your own actions. And they were both so nice and kind, it was a pleasure to be near them. So I was almost thankful for that horrid accident, which had cut the Gordian knot of my perplexity as to a house to lodge in.

It was a fortnight before I was well enough to get out of bed and lie comfortably on the sofa. All that time

Jack and Elsie tended me with unsparing devotion. Elsie had a little bed made up in my room; and Jack came to see me two or three times a day, and sat for whole hours with me. It was so nice he was a doctor! A doctor, you know, isn't a man - in some ways. And it soothed me so to have him sitting there with Elsie by my bedside.

They were "Jack" and "Elsie" to me, to their faces, before three days were out; and I was plain "Una" to them: it sounded so sweet and sisterly. Elsie slipped it out the second morning as naturally as could be.

"Una'd like a cup of tea, Jack;" then as red as fire all at once, she corrected herself, and added, "I mean, Miss Callingham."

"Oh, do call me Una!" I cried; "it's so much nicer and more natural.... But how did you come to know my name was Una at all?" For she slipped it out as glibly as if she'd always called me so.

"Why, everybody knows that." Elsie answered, amused. "The whole world speaks of you always as Una Callingham. You forget you're a celebrity. Doctors have read memoirs about you at Medical Congresses. You've been discussed in every paper in Europe and America."

I paused and sighed. This was very humiliating. It was unpleasant to rank in the public mind somewhere between Constance Kent and Laura Bridgman. But I had to put up with it.

"Very well," I said, with a deep breath, "if those I don't care for call me so behind my back, let me at least have the pleasure of hearing myself called so by those I love, like you, Elsie."

She leant over me and kissed my forehead with a burst of genuine delight.

"Then you love me, Una!" she exclaimed.

"How can I help it?" I answered. "I love you dearly already." And I might have added with truth, "And your brother also."

For Jack was really, without any exception, the most lovable man I ever met in my life - at once so strong and manly, and yet so womanly and so gentle. Every day I stopped there, I liked him better and better. I was glad when he came into my room, and sorry when he went away again to work on the farm: for he worked very hard; his hand was all horny with common agricultural labour. It was sad to think of such a man having to do such work. And yet he was so clever, and such a capital doctor. I wondered he hadn't done well and stayed in England. But Elsie told me he'd had great disappointments, and failed in his profession through no fault of his own. I could never understand that: he had such a delightful manner. Though, perhaps I was prejudiced; for, in point of fact, I began to feel I was really in love with Jack Cheriton.

And Jack was in love with me too. This was a curious result of my voyage to Canada in search of Dr. Ivor! Instead of hunting up the criminal, I had stopped to fall in love with one of his friends and neighbours. And I found it so delicious: I won't pretend to deny it. I was absolutely happy when Jack sat by my bedside and held my hand in his. I didn't know what it would lead to, or whether it would ever lead to anything at all; but I was happy meanwhile just to love and be loved by him. I think when you're really in love, that's quite enough. Jack never proposed to me: he never asked me to marry him. He just sat by my bedside and held my hand; and once, when Elsie went out to fetch my beef-tea, he stooped hastily down and kissed, me, oh, so tenderly! I don't know why, but I wasn't the least surprised. It seemed to me quite natural that Jack should kiss me.

So I went idly on for a fortnight, in a sort of lazy lotus-land, never thinking of the future, but as happy and as much at home as if I'd lived all my life with Jack and Elsie. I hated even to think I would soon be well; for then I'd have to go and look out for Courtenay Ivor.

At last one afternoon I was sufficiently strong to be lifted out of bed, and dressed in a morning robe, and laid out on the sofa in the little drawing-room. It looked out upon the verandah, which was high above the ground; and Jack came in and sat with me, alone without Elsie. My heart throbbed high at that: I liked to be alone for half-an-hour with Jack. Perhaps... But who knows? Well, at any rate, even if he didn't, it was nice to have the chance of a good long, quiet chat with him. I loved Elsie dearly; but at a moment like this, why, I liked to have Jack all to myself without even Elsie.

So I was pleased when Jack told me Elsie was going into Palmyra with the buggy to get the English letters. Then she'd be gone a good long time! Oh, how lovely! How beautiful!

"Is there anything you'd like from the town?" he asked, as Elsie drove past the window. "Anything Elsie could get for you? If so, please say so."

I hesitated a moment.

"Do you think," I asked at last, for I didn't want to be troublesome, "she could get me a lemon?"

"Oh, certainly," Jack answered; "there she goes in the buggy! Here, wait a moment, Una! I'll run after her to the gate this minute and tell her."

He sprang lightly on to the parapet of the verandah. Then, with one hand held behind him to poise himself, palm open backward, he leapt with a bound to the road, and darted after her hurriedly.

My heart stood still within me. That action revealed him. The back, the open hand, the gesture, the bend - I would have known them anywhere. With a horrible revulsion I recognised the truth. This was my father's murderer! This was Courtenay Ivor!

CHAPTER XVIII.

MURDER WILL OUT

He was gone but for three minutes. Meanwhile, I buried my face in my burning hands, and cried to myself in unspeakable misery.

For, horrible as it sounds to say so, I knew perfectly well now that Jack was Dr. Ivor: yet, in spite of that knowledge, I loved him still. He was my father's murderer; and I couldn't help loving him!

It was that that filled up the cup of my misery to overflowing. I loved the man well: and I must turn to denounce him.

He came back, flushed and hot, expecting thanks for his pains.

"Well, she'll get you the lemon, Una," he said, panting. "I overtook her by the big tulip-tree."

I gazed at him fixedly, taking my hands from my face, with the tears still wet on my burning cheek.

"You've deceived me!" I cried sternly. "Jack, you've given me a false name. I know who you are, now. You're no Jack at all. You're Courtenay Ivor!"

He drew back, quite amazed. Yet he didn't seem thunderstruck. Not fear but surprise was the leading note on his features.

"So you've found that out at last, Una!" he exclaimed, staring hard at me. "Then you remember me after all, darling! You know who I am. You haven't quite forgotten me. And you recall what has gone, do you?"

I rose from the sofa, ill as I was, in my horror.

"You dare to speak to me like that, sir!" I cried. "You, whom I've tracked out to your hiding-place and discovered! You, whom I've come across the ocean to hunt down! You, whom I mean to give up this very day to Justice! Let me go from your house at once! How dare you ever bring me here? How dare you stand unabashed before the daughter of the man you so cruelly murdered?"

He drew back like one stung.

"The daughter of the man I murdered!" he faltered out slowly, as in a turmoil of astonishment. "The man _I_ murdered! Oh, Una, is it possible you've forgotten so much, and yet remember me myself? I can't believe it, darling. Sit down, my child, and think. Surely, surely the rest will come back to you gradually."

His calmness unnerved me. What could he mean by these words? No actor on earth could dissemble like this. His whole manner was utterly unlike the manner of a man just detected in a terrible crime. He seemed rather to reproach me, indeed, than to crouch; to be shocked and indignant.

"Explain yourself," I said coldly, in a very chilly voice. "Courtenay Ivor, I give you three minutes to explain. At the end of that time, if you can't exonerate yourself, I walk out of this house to give you up, as I ought, to the arm of Justice!"

He looked at me, all pity, yet inexpressibly reproachful.

"Oh, Una," he cried, clasping his hands - those small white hands of his - Aunt Emma's hands - the murderer's hands - how had I never before noticed them? - "and I, who have suffered so much for you! I, who have wrecked my whole life for you, ungrudgingly, willingly! I, who have sacrificed even Elsie's happiness and Elsie's future for you! This is too, too hard! Una, Una, spare me!"

A strange trembling seized me. It was in my heart to rush forward and clasp him to my breast. Murderer or no murderer, his look, his voice, cut me sharply to the heart. Words trembled on the tip of my tongue: "Oh, Jack, I love you!" But with a violent effort, I repressed them sternly. This horrible revulsion seemed to tear me in two. I loved him so much. Though till the moment of the discovery, I never quite realised how deeply I loved him.

"Courtenay Ivor," I said slowly, steeling myself once more for a hard effort, "I knew who you were at once when I saw you poise yourself on the parapet. Once before in my life I saw you like that, and the picture it produced has burned itself into the very fibre and marrow of my being. As long as I live, I can never get rid of it. It was when you leapt from the window at The Grange, at Woodbury, after murdering my father!"

He started once more.

"Una," he said solemnly, in a very clear voice, "there's some terrible error somewhere. You're utterly mistaken about what took place that night. But oh, great heavens! how am I ever to explain the misconception to YOU? If you still think thus, it would be cruel to undeceive you. I daren't tell you the whole truth. It would kill you! It would kill you!"

I drew myself up like a pillar of ice.

"Go on," I said, in a hard voice; for I saw he had something to say. "Don't mind for my heart. Tell me the truth. I can stand it."

He hesitated for a minute or two.

"I can't!" he cried huskily. "Dear Una, don't ask me! Won't you trust me, without? Won't you believe me when I tell you, I never did it?"

"No, I can't," I answered with sullen resolution, though my eyes belied my words. "I can't disbelieve the evidence of my own senses. I SAW you escape that night. I see you still. I've seen you for years. I KNOW it was you, and you only, who did it!"

He flung himself down in a chair, and let his arms drop listlessly.

"Oh! what can I ever do to disillusion you?" he cried in despair. "Oh! what can I ever do? This is too, too terrible!"

I moved towards the door.

"I'm going," I said, with a gulp. "You've deceived me, Jack. You've lied to me. You have given me feigned names. You have decoyed me to your house under false pretences. And I recognise you now. I know you in all your baseness. You're my father's murderer! Don't hope to escape by playing on my feelings. I'd deserve to be murdered myself, if I could act like that! I'm on my way to the police-office, to give you in custody on the charge of murdering Vivian Callingham at Woodbury!"

He jumped up again, all anxiety.

"Oh, no, you mustn't walk!" he cried, laying his hand upon my arm. "Give me up, if you like; but wait till the buggy comes back, and Elsie'll drive you round with me. You're not fit to go a step as you are at present... Oh! what shall I ever do, though. You're so weak and ill. Elsie'll never allow it."

"Elsie'll never allow WHAT?" I asked; though I felt it was rather more grotesque than undignified and inconsistent thus to parley and make terms with my father's murderer. Though, to be sure, it was Jack, and I couldn't bear to refuse him.

He kept his hand on my arm with an air of authority.

"Una, my child," he said, thrusting me back - and even at that moment of supreme horror, a thrill ran all through my body at his touch and his words - "you MUSTN'T go out of this house as you are this minute. I refuse to allow it. I'm your doctor, and I forbid it. You're under my charge, and I won't let you stir. If I did, I'd be responsible."

He pushed me gently into a chair.

"I gave you but one false name," he said slowly - "the name of Cheriton. To be sure I, was never christened John, but I'm Jack to my intimates. It was my nickname from a baby. Jack's what I've always been called at home - Jack's what, in the dear old days at Torquay, you always called me. But I saw if I let you know who I was at once, there'd be no chance of recalling the past, and so saving you from yourself. To save you, I consented to that one mild deception. It succeeded in bringing you here, and in keeping you here till Elsie and I were once more what we'd always been to you. I meant to tell you all in the end, when the right time came. Now, you've forced my hand, and I don't know how I can any longer refrain from telling you."

"Telling me WHAT?" I said icily. "What do you mean by your words? Why all these dark hints? If you've anything to say, why not say it like a man?"

For I loved him so much that in my heart of hearts, I half hoped there might still be some excuse, some explanation.

He looked at me solemnly. Then he leant back in his chair and drew his hand across his brow. I could see now why I hadn't recognised that delicate hand before: white as it was by nature, hard work on the farm had long bronzed and distorted it. But I saw also, for the first time, that the palm was scarred with cuts and rents - exactly like Minnie Moore's, exactly like Aunt Emma's.

"Una," he began slowly, in a very puzzled tone, "if I

could, I'd give myself up and be tried, and be found guilty and executed for your sake, sooner than cause you any further distress, or expose you to the shock of any more disclosures. But I can't do that, on Elsie's account. Even if I decided to put Elsie to that shame and disgrace - which would hardly be just, which would hardly be manly of me - Elsie knows all, and Elsie'd never consent to it. She'd never let her brother be hanged for a crime of which (as she knows) he's entirely innocent. And she'd tell out all in full court - every fact, every detail - which would be worse for you ten thousand times in the end than learning it here quietly."

"Tell me all," I said, growing stony, yet trembling from head to foot. "Oh, Jack," - I seized his hand, - "I don't know what you mean! But I somehow trust you. I want to know all. I can bear anything - anything - better than this suspense. You MUST tell me! You MUST explain to me!"

"I will," he said slowly, looking hard into my eyes, and feeling my pulse half unconsciously with his finger as he spoke. "Una darling, you must make up your mind now for a terrible shock. I won't tell you in words, for you'd never believe it. I'll SHOW you who it was that fired the shot at Mr. Callingham."

He moved over to the other side of the room, and unlocking drawer after drawer, took a bundle of photographs from the inmost secret cabinet of a desk in the corner.

"There, Una," he said, selecting one of them and holding it up before my eyes. "Prepare yourself, darling. That's the person who pulled the trigger that night in the library!"

I looked at it and fell back with a deadly shriek of horror. It was an instantaneous photograph. It represented a scene just before the one the Inspector gave me. And there, in its midst, I saw myself as a girl, with a pistol in my hand. The muzzle flashed and smoked. I knew the whole truth. It was I myself who held the pistol and fired at my father!

CHAPTER XIX.

THE REAL MURDERER

For some seconds I sat there, leaning back in my chair and gazing close at that incredible, that accusing document. I knew it couldn't lie: I knew it must be the very handiwork of unerring Nature. Then slowly a recollection began to grow up in my mind. I knew of my own memory it was really true. I remembered it so, now, as in a glass, darkly. I remembered having stood, with the pistol in my hand, pointing it straight at the breast of the man with the long white beard whom they called my father. A new mental picture rose up before me like a vision. I remembered it all as something that once really occurred to me.

Yet I remembered it, as I had long remembered the next scene in the series, merely as so much isolated and unrelated fact, without connection of any sort to link it to the events that preceded or followed it. It was *I* who shot my father! I realised that now with a horrid gulp. But what on earth did I ever shoot him for? And I had hunted down Jack for the crime I had committed myself! I had threatened to give him up for my own dreadful parricide!

After a minute, I rose, and staggered feebly to the door. I saw the path of duty clear as daylight before me.

"Where are you going?" Jack faltered out, watching me close with anxious eyes, lest I should stumble or faint.

And I answered aloud, in a hollow voice:

"To the police-station, of course, - to give myself into custody for the murder of my father."

When I thought it was Jack, though I loved him better than I loved my own life, I would have given him up to justice as a sacred duty. Now I knew it was myself, how could I possibly do otherwise? How could I love my own life better than I loved dear Jack's, who had given up everything to save me and protect me?

With a wild bound of horror, Jack sprang upon me at once. He seized me bodily in his arms. He carried me back into the room with irresistible strength. I fought against him in vain. He laid me on the sofa. He bent over me like a whirlwind and smothered me with hot kisses.

"My darling," he cried, "my darling, then this shock hasn't killed you! It hasn't stunned you like the last! You're still your own dear self! You've still strength to think and plan exactly what one would expect from you. Oh! Una, my Una, you must wait and hear all. When you've learned HOW it happened, you won't wish to act so rashly."

I struggled to free myself, though his arms were hard and close like a strong man's around me.

"Let me go, Jack!" I cried feebly, trying to tear myself from his grasp. "I love you better than I love my own life. If I would have given YOU up, how much more must I give up myself, now I know it was I who really did it!"

He held me down by main force. He pinned me to the sofa. I suppose it's because I'm a woman, and weak, and all that - but I liked even then to feel how strong and how big he was, and how feeble I was myself, like a child in his arms. And I resisted on purpose, just to feel him hold me. Somehow, I couldn't realize, after all, that I was indeed a murderess. It didn't seem possible. I couldn't believe it was in me.

"Jack," I said slowly, giving way at last, and letting him hold me down with his small strong hands and slender iron wrist, "tell me, if you will, how I came to do it. I'll sit here quite still, if only you'll tell me. Am I really a murderess?"

Jack recoiled like one shot.

"YOU a murderess, my spotless Una!" he exclaimed, all aghast. "If anyone else on earth but you had just asked such a thing in my presence, I'd have leapt at the fellow's throat, and held him down till I choked him!"

"But I did it!" I cried wildly. "I remember now, I did it. It all comes back to me at last. I fired at him, just so. I aimed the loaded pistol point-blank at his heart, I can hear the din in my ears. I can see the flash at the muzzle. And then I flung down the pistol - like this - at my feet: and darkness came on; and I forgot everything. Why, Dr. Marten knew that much! I remember now, he told me he'd formed a very strong impression, from the nature of the wound and the position of the various objects on the floor of the room, who it was that did it! He must have seen it was *I* who flung down the pistol."

Jack gazed at me in suspense.

"He's a very good friend of yours, then," he murmured, "that Dr. Marten. For he never said a word of all that at the inquest."

"But I must give myself up!" I cried, in a fever of penitence for what that other woman who once was ME had done. "Oh, Jack, do let me! It's hateful to know I'm a murderess and to go unpunished. It's hateful to draw back from the fate I'd have imposed on another. I'd like to be hanged for it. I want to be hanged. It's the only possible way to appease one's conscience."

And yet, though I said it, I felt all the time it wasn't really I, but that other strange girl who once lived at The Grange and looked exactly like me. I remember it, to be sure; but it was in my Other State: and, so far as my moral responsibility was concerned, my Other State and I were two different people.

For I knew in my heart I couldn't commit a murder.

Jack rose without a word, and fetched me in some brandy.

"Drink this," he said calmly, in his authoritative medical tone; "drink this before you say another sentence."

And, obedient to his order, I took it up and drank it.

Then he sat down beside me, and took my hand in his,

and with very gentle words began to reason and argue with me.

He was glad I'd struggled, he said, because that broke the first force of the terrible shock for me. Action was always good for one in any great crisis. It gave an outlet for the pent-up emotions, too suddenly let loose with explosive force, and kept them from turning inward and doing serious harm, as mine had done on that horrible night of the accident. He called it always the accident, I noticed, and never the murder. That gave me fresh hope. Could I really after all have fired unintentionally? But no; when I came to look inward, - to look backward on my past state, - I was conscious all the time of some strong and fierce resentment smouldering deep in my heart at the exact moment of firing. However it might have happened, I was angry with the man with the long white beard: I fired at him hastily, it is true, but with malice prepense and deliberate intent to wound and hurt him.

Jack went on, however, undeterred, in a low and quiet voice, soothing my hand with his as he spoke, and very kind and gentle. My spirit rebelled at the thought that I could ever for one moment have imagined him a murderer. I said so in one wild burst. Jack held my hand, and still reasoned with me. I like a man's reasoning; it's so calm and impartial. It seems to overcome one by its mere display of strength. If I'd changed my mind once, Jack said, I might change it again, when further evidence on the point was again forthcoming. I mustn't give myself up to the police till I understood much more. If I did, I would commit a very grave mistake. There were reasons that had led to the firing of the shot. Very grave reasons too. Couldn't I restore and reconstruct them, now I knew the last stage of the terrible history? If possible, he'd rather I should arrive at them by myself than that he should tell me.

I cast my mind back all in vain.

"No, Jack," I said trustfully. "I can't remember anything one bit like that. I can remember forward, sometimes, but never backwards. I can remember now how I flung down the pistol, and how the servants burst in. But not a word, not an item, of what went before. That's all a pure blank to me."

And then I went on to tell him in very brief outline how the first thing I could recollect in all my life was the Australian scene with the big blue-gum-trees; and how that had been recalled to me by the picture at Jane's; and how one scene in that way had gradually suggested another; and how I could often think ahead from a given fact but never go back behind it and discover what led up to it.

Jack drew his hand over his chin and reflected silently.

"That's odd," he said, after a pause. "Yet very compre-hensible. I might almost have thought of that before: might have arrived at it on general principles. Psychologically and physiologically it's exactly what one would have expected from the nature of memory. And yet it never occurred to me. Set up the train of thought in the order in which it originally presented itself, and the links may readily restore themselves in successive series. Try to trace it backward in the inverse order, and the process is very much more difficult and involved. - Well, we'll try things just so with you, Una. We'll begin by reconstructing your first life as far as we can from the very outset, with the aid of these stray hints of yours; and then we'll see whether we can get you to remember all your past up to the day of the accident more easily."

I gazed up at him with gratitude.

"Oh, Jack," I said, trembling, "in spite of this shock, I believe I can do it now. I believe I can remember. The scales are falling from my eyes. I'm becoming myself again. What you've said and what you've shown me seems to have broken down a veil. I feel as if I could reconstruct all now, when once the key's suggested to me."

He smiled at me encouragingly. Oh, how could I ever have doubted him?

"That's right, darling," he answered. "I should have expected as much, indeed. For now for the very first time since the accident you've got really at the other side of the great blank in your memory."

I felt so happy, though I knew I was a murderess. I didn't mind now whether I was hanged or not. To love Jack and be loved by him was quite enough for me. When he called me "darling," I was in the seventh heavens. It sounded so familiar. I knew he must have called me so, often and often before, in the dim dead past that was just beginning to recur to me.

Grant Allen

CHAPTER XX.

THE STRANGER FROM THE SEA

I held his hand tight. It was so pleasant to know I could love him now with a clear conscience, even if I had to give myself up to the police to-morrow. And indeed, being a woman, I didn't really much care whether they took me or not, if only I could love Jack, and know Jack loved me.

"You must tell me everything - this minute - Jack," I said, clinging to him like a child. "I can't bear this suspense. Begin telling me at once. You'll do me more harm than good if you keep me waiting any longer."

Jack took instinctively a medical view of the situation.

"So I think, my child," he said, looking lovingly at me. "Your nerves are on the rack, and will be the better for unstringing. Oh, Una, it's such a comfort that you know at last who I am! It's such a comfort that I'm able to talk to you to-day just as we two used to talk four years ago in Devonshire!"

"Did I love you then, Jack?" I whispered, nestling still closer to him, in spite of my horror. Or rather, my very horror made me feel more acutely than ever the need for protection. I was no longer alone in the world. I had a man to support me.

"You told me so, darling," he answered, smoothing my hair with his hand. "Have you forgotten all about it? Doesn't even that come back? Can't you remember it now, when I've told you who I am and how it all happened?"

I shook my head.

"All cloudy still," I replied, vaguely. "Some dim sense of familiarity, perhaps, - as when people say they have a feeling of having lived all this over somewhere else before, - but nothing more certain, nothing more definite."

"Then I must begin at the beginning," Jack answered, bracing himself for his hard task, "and reconstruct your whole life for you, as far as I know it, from your very childhood. I'm particularly anxious you should not merely be TOLD what took place, but should remember the past. There are gaps in my own knowledge I want you to eke out. There are places I want you to help me myself over. And besides, it'll be more satisfactory to yourself to remember than to be told it."

I leaned back, almost exhausted. Incredible as it may seem to you, in spite of that awful photograph, I couldn't really believe even so I had killed my father. And yet I knew very well now that Jack, at least, hadn't done it. That was almost enough. But not quite. My head swam round in terror. I waited and longed for Jack to explain the whole thing to me.

"You remember," he said, watching me close, "that

when you lived as a very little girl in Australia you had a papa who seems different to you still from the papa in your later childish memories?"

"I remember it very well," I replied. "It came back to me on the Sarmatian. I think of him always now as the papa in the loose white linen coat. The more I dwell on him, the more does he come out to me as a different man from the other one - the father...I shot at The Grange, at Woodbury. The father that lives with me in that ineffaceable Picture."

"He WAS a different man," Jack answered, with a sudden burst, as if he knew all my story. "Una, I may as well relieve your mind all at once on that formidable point. You shot that man" - he pointed to the white-bearded person in the photograph, - "but it was not parricide: it was not even murder. It was under grave provocation...in more than self-defence...and he was NOT your father."

"Not my father!" I cried, clasping my hands and leaning forward in my profound suspense. "But I killed him all the same! Oh, Jack, how terrible!"

"You must quiet yourself, my child," he said, still soothing me automatically. "I want your aid in this matter. You must listen to me calmly, and bring your mind to bear on all I say to you."

Then he began with a regular history of my early life, which came back to me as fast as he spoke, scene by scene and year by year, in long and familiar succession. I remembered everything, sometimes only when he suggested it; but sometimes also, before he said the words, my memory outran his tongue, and I put in a recollection or two with my own tongue as they recurred to me under the stimulus of this new birth of my dead nature. I recalled my early days in the far bush in Australia; my journey home to England on the big steamer with mamma; the way we travelled about for years from place to place on the Continent. I remembered how I had been strictly enjoined, too, never to speak of baby; and how my father used to watch my mother just as closely as he watched me, always afraid, as it appeared to me, she should make some verbal slip or let out some great secret in an unguarded moment. He seemed relieved, I recollected now, when my poor mother died: he grew less strict with me then, but as far as I could judge, though he was careful of my health, he never really loved me.

Then Jack reminded me further of other scenes that came much later in my forgotten life. He reminded me of my trip to Torquay, where I first met him: and all at once the whole history of my old visits to the Moores came back like a flood to me. The memory seemed to inundate and overwhelm my brain. They were the happiest time of all life, those delightful visits, when I met Jack and fell in love with him, and half confided my love to my Cousin Minnie. Strange to say, though at Torquay itself I'd forgotten it all, in that little Canadian house, with Jack by my side to recall it, it rushed back like a wave upon me. I'd fallen in love with Jack without my father's knowledge or consent; and I knew very well my father would never allow me to marry him. He had ideas of his own, my father, about the sort of person I ought to marry: and I half suspected in my heart of hearts he meant if possible always to keep me at home single to take care of him and look after him. I didn't know, as yet, he had sufficient reasons of his own for desiring me to remain for ever unmarried.

I remembered, too, that I never really loved my father. His nature was hard, cold, reserved, unsympathetic. I only feared and obeyed him. At times, my own strong character came out, I remembered, and I defied him to his face, defied him openly. Then there were scenes in the house, dreadful scenes, too hateful to dwell upon: and the servants came up to my room at the end and comforted me.

So, step by step, Jack reminded me of everything in my own past life, up to the very night of the murder, from which my Second State dated. I'd come back from Torquay a week or two before, very full indeed of Jack, and determined at all costs, sooner or later, to marry him. But though I had kept all quiet, papa had suspected my liking on the day of the Berry Pomeroy athletics, and had forbidden me to see Jack, or to write to him, or to have anything further to say to him. He was determined, he told me, whoever I married, I shouldn't at least marry a beggarly doctor. All that I remembered; and also how, in spite of the prohibition, I wrote letters to Jack, but could receive none in return - lest my father should see them.

And still, the central mystery of the murder was no nearer solution. I held my breath in terror. Had I really any sort of justification in killing him?

Dimly and instinctively, as Jack went on, a faint sense of resentment and righteous indignation against the man with the white beard rose up vaguely in my mind by slow degrees. I knew I had been angry with him, I knew I had defied him, but how or why as yet I knew not.

Then Jack suddenly paused, and began in a different voice a new part of his tale. It was nothing I remembered or could possibly remember, he said; but it was necessary to the comprehension of what came after, and would help me to recall it. About a week after I left Torquay, it seemed, Jack was in his consulting-room at Babbicombe one day, having just returned from a very long bicycle ride - for he was a first-rate cyclist, - when the servant announced a new patient; and a very worn-out old man came in to visit him.

The man had a ragged grey beard and scanty white hair; he was clad in poor clothes, and had tramped on foot all the way from London to Babbicombe, where Jack used to practice. But Jack saw at once under this rough exterior he had the voice and address of a cultivated gentleman, though he was so broken down by want and long suffering and exposure and illness that he looked like a beggar just let loose from the workhouse.

I held my breath as Jack showed me the poor old man's photograph. It was a portrait taken after death - for Jack attended him to the end through a fatal illness; - and it showed a face thin and worn, and much lined by unspeakable hardships. But I burst out crying at once the very moment I looked at it. For a second or two, I couldn't say why: I suppose it was instinct. Blood is thicker than water, they tell us; and I have the intuition of kindred very strong in me, I believe. But at any rate, I cried silently, with big hot tears, while I looked at that dead face of silent suffering, as I never had cried over the photograph of the respectable-looking man who lay dead on the floor of the library, and whom I was always taught to consider my father. Then it came back to me, why... I gazed at it and grew faint. I clutched Jack's arm for support. I knew what it meant now. The poor worn old man who lay dead on the bed with that look of mute agony on his features - was my first papa: the papa in the loose white linen coat: the one I remembered with childlike love and trustfulness in my earliest babyish Australian recollections!

I couldn't mistake the face. It was burnt into my brain now. This was he, though much older and sadder, and more scarred and lined by age and weather. It was my very first papa. My own papa. I cried silently still. I couldn't bear to look at it. Then the real truth broke upon me once more. This, and this alone, was in very deed my one real father!

I seized the faded photograph and pressed it to my lips.

"Oh, I know him!" I cried wildly. "It's my father! My father!"

Some minutes passed before Jack could go on with his story. This rush of emotions was too much for me for a while. I could hardly hear him or attend to him, so deeply did it stir me.

At last I calmed down, still holding that pathetic photograph on the table before me.

"Tell me all about him," I murmured, sobbing. "For, Jack, I remember now, he was so good and kind, and I loved him - I loved him."

Jack went on with his story, trying to soothe me and reassure me. The old man introduced himself by very cautious degrees as a person in want, not so much of money, though of that to be sure he had none, as of kindness and sympathy in a very great sorrow. He was a shipwrecked mariner, in a sense: shipwrecked on the sea of Life and on the open Pacific as well. But once he had been a clergyman, and a man of education, position, reputation, fortune.

Gradually as he went on Jack began to grasp at the truth of this curious tale. The worn and battered stranger had but lately landed in London from a sailing vessel which had brought him over from a remote Pacific islet: not a tropical islet of the kind with whose palms and parrots we are all so familiar, but a cold and snowy rock, away off far south, among the frosts and icebergs, near the Antarctic continent. There for twenty long years that unhappy man had lived by himself a solitary life.

I started at the sound.

"For twenty years!" I exclaimed. "Oh, Jack, you must be wrong; for how could that be? I was only eighteen when all this happened. How could my real father have been twenty years away from me, when I was only eighteen, and I remember him so perfectly?"

Jack looked at me and shook his head.

"You've much to learn yet, Una," he answered. "The story's a long one. You were NOT eighteen but twenty-two at the time. You've been deliberately misled as to your own age all along. You developed late, and were always short for your real years, not tall and preco-cious as we all of us imagined. But you were four years older than Mr. Callingham pretended. You're twenty-six now, not twenty-two as you think. Wait, and in time you'll hear all about it."

He went on with his story. I listened, spell-bound. The unhappy man explained to Jack how he had been wrecked on the voyage, and escaped on a raft with one other passenger: how they had drifted far south, before waves and current, till they were cast at last on this wretched island: how they remained there for a month or two, picking up a precarious living on roots and berries and eggs of sea-birds: and how at last, one day, he had come back from hunting limpets and sea-urchins on the shore of a lonely bay - to find, to his amazement, his companion gone, and himself left alone on that desolate island. His fellow-castaway, he knew then, had deceived and deserted him!

There was no room, indeed, to doubt the treachery of the wretched being who had so basely treated him. As he looked, a ship under full sail stood away to north-ward. In vain the unhappy man made wild signals from the shore with his tattered garments. No notice was taken of them. His companion must deliberately have suppressed the other's existence, and pretended to be alone by himself on the island.

"And his name?" Jack asked of the poor old man, horrified.

The stranger answered without a moment's pause:

"His name, if you want it - was Vivian Callingham."

"And yours?" Jack continued, as soon as he could recover from his first shock of horror.

"And mine," the poor castaway replied, "is Richard Wharton."

As Jack told me those words, another strange thrill ran through me.

"Richard Wharton was the name of mamma's first husband. Then I'm not a Callingham at all!" I cried, unable to take it all in at first in its full complexity. "I'm really a Wharton!"

Jack nodded his head in assent.

"Yes, you're really a Wharton," he said. "You're the baby that died, as we all were told. Your true Christian name's Mary. But, Una, you were always Una to all of us in England; and though the real Una Callingham died when you were a little girl of three or four years old, you'll be Una always now to Elsie and me. We can't think of you as other than we've always called you."

Then he went on to explain to me how the stranger had landed in London, alone and friendless, twenty years later, from a passing Australian merchant vessel which had picked him up on the island. All those years he had waited, and fed himself on eggs of penguins. He landed by himself, the crew having given him a suit of old clothes, and subscribed to find him in immediate necessaries. He began to inquire cautiously in London about his wife and family. At first, he could learn little or nothing; for nobody remembered him, and he feared to ask too openly, a sort of Enoch Arden terror restraining him from proclaiming his personality till he knew exactly what had happened in his long absence. But bit by bit, he found out at last that his wife had married again, and was now long dead: and that the man she had married was Vivian Callingham, his own treacherous companion on the Crozet Islands. As soon as he learned that, the full depth of the man's guilt burst upon him like a thunderbolt. Richard Wharton understood now why Vivian Callingham had left him alone on those desert rocks, and sailed away in the ship without telling the captain of his fellow-castaway's plight. He saw the whole vile plot the man had concocted at once, and the steps he had taken to carry it into execution.

Vivian Callingham, whom I falsely thought my father, had gone back to Australia with pretended news of Richard Wharton's death. He had sought my widowed mother in her own home up country, and told her a lying tale of his devotion to her husband in his dying moments on that remote ocean speck in the far Southern Pacific. By this story he ingratiated himself. He knew she was rich: he knew she was worth marrying: and to marry her, he had left my own real father, Richard Wharton, to starve and languish for twenty years among rocks and sea-fowl on a lonely island!

My blood ran cold at such a tale of deadly treachery. I remembered now to have heard some small part of it before. But much of it, as Jack told it to me, was quite new and unexpected. No wonder I had turned in horror that night from the man I long believed to be my own father, when I learned by what vile and cruelly treacherous means he had succeeded in imposing his supposed relationship upon me! But still, all this brought me no nearer the real question of questions - why did I shoot him?

CHAPTER XXI.

THE PLOT UNRAVELS ITSELF

As Jack went on unfolding that strange tale of fraud and heartless wrong, my interest every moment grew more and more absorbing. But I can't recall it now exactly as Jack told me it. I can only give you the substance of that terrible story.

When Richard Wharton first learned of his wife's second marriage during his own lifetime to that wicked wretch who had ousted and supplanted him, he believed also, on the strength of Vivian Callingham's pretences, that his own daughter had died in her babyhood in Australia. He fancied, therefore, that no person of his kin remained alive at all, and that he might proceed to denounce and punish Vivian Callingham. With that object in view, he tramped down all the way from London to Torquay, to make himself known to his wife's relations, the Moores, and to their cousin, Courtenay Ivor of Babbicombe - my Jack, as I called him. For various reasons of his own, he called first on Jack, and proceeded to detail to him this terrible family story.

At first hearing, Jack could hardly believe such a tale was true - of his Una's father, as he still thought Vivian Callingham. But a strange chance happened to reveal a still further complication. It came out in this way. I had given Jack a recent photograph of myself in fancy dress, which hung up over his mantelpiece. As the weather-worn visitor's eye fell on the picture, he started and grew pale.

"Why, that's her!" he cried with a sudden gasp. "That's my daughter - Mary Wharton!"

Well, naturally enough Jack thought, to begin with, this was a mere mistake on his strange visitor's part.

"That's her half-sister," he said, "Una Callingham - your wife's child by her second marriage. She may be like her, no doubt, as half-sisters often are. But Mary Wharton, I know, died some eighteen years ago or so, when Una was quite a baby, I believe. I've heard all about it, because, don't you see, I'm engaged to Una."

The poor wreck of a clergyman, however, shook his head with profound conviction. He knew better than that.

"Oh no," he said decisively: "that's my child, Mary Wharton. Even after all these years, I couldn't possibly be mistaken. Blood is thicker than water: I'd know her among ten thousand. She'd be just that age now, too. I see the creature's vile plot. His daughter died young, and he's palmed off my Mary as his own child, to keep her money in his hands. But never mind the money. Thank Heaven, she's alive! That's her! That's my Mary!"

The plot seemed too diabolical and too improbable for anybody to believe. Jack could hardly think it possible when his new friend told him. But the stranger persisted so - it's hard for me even to think of him as quite really my father - that Jack at last brought out two or three earlier photographs I'd given him some time before; and his visitor recognised them at once, in all their stages, as his own daughter. This roused Jack's curiosity. He determined to hunt the matter up with his unknown connection. And he hunted it up thenceforward with deliberate care, till he proved every word of it.

Meanwhile, the poor broken-down man, worn out with his long tramp and his terrible emotions, fell ill almost at once, in Jack's own house, and became rapidly so feeble that Jack dared not question him further. The return to civilisation was more fatal than his long solitary banishment. At the end of a week he died, leaving on Jack's mind a profound conviction that all he had said was true, and that I was really Richard Wharton's daughter, not Vivian Callingham's.

"For a week or two I made inquiries, Una," Jack said to me as we sat there, - "inquiries which I won't detail to you in full just now, but which gradually showed me the truth of the poor soul's belief. What you yourself told me just now chimes in exactly with what I discovered elsewhere, by inquiry and by letters from Australia. The baby that died was the real Una Callingham. Shortly after its death, your stepfather and your mother left the colony. All your real father's money had been bequeathed to his child: and your mother's also was settled on you. Mr. Callingham saw that if your mother died, and you lived and married, he himself would be deprived of the fortune for which he had so wickedly plotted. So he made up another plot even more extraordinary and more diabolical still than the first. He decided to pretend it was Mary Wharton that died, and to palm you off on the world as his own child, Una Callingham. For if Mary Wharton died, the property at once became absolutely your mother's, and she could will it away to her husband or anyone else she chose to."

"But baby was so much younger than I!" I cried, going back on my recollections once more. "How could he ever manage to make the dates come right again?"

"Quite true," Jack answered; "the baby was younger than you. But your step-father - I've no other name by which I can call him - made a clever plan to set that straight. He concealed from the people in Australia which child had been ill, and he entered her death as Mary Wharton. Then, to cover the falsification, he left Melbourne at once, and travelled about for some years on the Continent in out-of-the-way places till all had been forgotten. You went forth upon the world as Una Callingham, with your true personality as Mary Wharton all obscured even in your own memory. Fortunately for your false father's plot, you were small for your age, and developed slowly: he gave out, on the contrary, that you were big for your years and had outgrown yourself, Australian-wise, both in wisdom and stature."

"But my mother!" I exclaimed, appalled. 'How could she ever consent to such a wicked deception?"

"Mr. Callingham had your mother completely under his thumb," Jack answered with promptitude. "She couldn't call her soul her own, your poor mother - so I've heard: he cajoled her and terrified her till she didn't dare to oppose him. Poor shrinking creature, she was afraid of her life to do anything except as he bade her.

He must have persuaded her first to acquiesce passively in this hateful plot, and then must have terrified her afterwards into full compliance by threats of exposure."

"He was a very unhappy man himself," I put in, casting back. "His money did him no good. I can remember now how gloomy and moody he was often, at The Grange."

"Quite true," Jack replied. "He lived in perpetual fear of your real father's return, or of some other break-down to his complicated system of successive deceptions. He never had a happy minute in his whole life, I believe. Blind terrors surrounded him. He was afraid of everything, and afraid of everybody. Only his scientific work seemed ever to give him any relief. There, he became a free man. He threw himself into that, heart and soul, on purpose, I fancy, because it absorbed him while he was at it, and prevented him for the time being from thinking of his position."

"And how did you find it all out?" I asked eagerly, anxious to get on to the end.

"Well, that's long to tell," Jack replied. "Too long for one sitting. I won't trouble you with it now. Discrepancies in facts and dates, and inquiries among servants both in England and in Victoria, first put me upon the track. But I said nothing at the time of my suspicions to anyone. I waited till I could appeal to the man's own conscience with success, as I hoped. And then, besides, I hardly knew how to act for the best. I wanted to marry you; and therefore, as far as was consistent with justice and honour, I wished to spare your supposed father a complete exposure."

"But why didn't you tell the police?" I asked.

"Because I had really nothing definite in any way to go upon. Realise the position to yourself, and you'll see how difficult it was for me. Mr. Callingham suspected I was paying you attentions. Clearly, under those circumstances, it was to my obvious interest that you should get possession of all his property. Any claims I might make for you would, therefore, be naturally regarded with suspicion. The shipwrecked man had told nobody but myself. I hadn't even an affidavit, a death-bed statement. All rested upon his word, and upon mine as retailing it. He was dead, and there was nothing but my narrative for what he told me. The story itself was too improbable to be believed by the police on such dubious evidence. I didn't even care to try. I wanted to make your step-father confess: and I waited for that till I could compel confession."

CHAPTER XXII.

MY MEMORY RETURNS

At last my chance came," Jack went on. "I'd found out almost everything; not, of course, exactly by way of legal proof, but to my own entire satisfaction: and I determined to lay the matter definitely at once before Mr. Callingham. So I took a holiday for a fortnight, to go bicycling in the Midlands I told my patients; and I fixed my head-quarters at Wrode, which, as you probably remember, is twenty miles off from Woodbury.

"It was important for my scheme I should catch Mr. Callingham alone. I had no idea of entrapping him. I wanted to work upon his conscience and induce him to confess. My object was rather to move him to remorse and restitution than to terrify or surprise him.

"So on the day of the accident - call it murder, if you will - I rode over on my machine, unannounced, to The Grange to see him. You knew where I was staying, you recollect -"

At the words, a burst of memory came suddenly over me.

"Oh yes!" I cried. "I remember. It was at the Wilsons',

184   Grant Allen

at Wrode. I wrote over there to tell you we were going to dine alone at six that evening, as papa had got his electric apparatus home from his instrument-maker, and was anxious to try his experiments early. You'd written to me privately - a boy brought the note - that you wanted to have an hour's talk alone with papa. I thought it was about ME, and I was, oh, ever so nervous!"

For it all came back to me now, as clear as yesterday.

Jack looked at me hard.

"I'm glad you remember that, dear," he said. "Now, Una, do try to remember all you can as I go along with my story... Well, I rode over alone, never telling anybody at Wrode where I was going, nor giving your step-father any reason of any sort to expect me. I trusted entirely to finding him busy with his new invention. When I reached The Grange, I came up the drive unperceived, and looking in at the library window, saw your father alone there. He was pottering over his chemicals. That gave me the clue. I left my bicycle under the window, tilted up against the wall, and walked in without ringing, going straight to the library. Nobody saw me come: nobody saw me return, except one old lady on the road, who seemed to have forgotten all about it by the time of the inquest."

(I nodded and gave a start. I knew that must have been Aunt Emma.)

"Except yourself, Una, no human soul on earth ever seemed to suspect me. And that wasn't odd; for you and your father, and perhaps Minnie Moore, were the only people in the world who ever knew I was in love with you or cared for you in any way."

"Go on," I said, breathless. "And you went into the library."

"I went into the library," Jack continued, "where I found your father, just returned from enjoying his cigar on the lawn. He was alone in the room -"

"No, no!" I cried eagerly, putting in my share now; for I had a part in the history. "He WASN'T alone, Jack, though you thought him so at the time. I remember all, at last. It comes back to me like a flash. Oh, heavens, how it comes back to me! Jack, Jack, I remember to-day every word, every syllable of it!"

He gazed at me in surprise.

"Then tell me yourself, Una!" he exclaimed. "How did you come to be there? For I knew you were there at last; but till you fired the pistol, I hadn't the faintest idea you had heard or seen anything. Tell me all about it, quick! There comes in MY mystery."

In one wild rush of thought the whole picture rose up like a vision before me.

"Why, Jack," I cried, "there was a screen, a little screen in the alcove! You remember the alcove at the west end of the room. It was so small a screen, you'd hardly have thought it could hide me; but it did - it did - and all, too, by accident. I'd gone in there after dinner, not much thinking where I went, and was seated on the floor by the little alcove window, reading a book by the twilight. It was a book papa told me I wasn't to read, and I took it trembling from the shelves, and was afraid he'd scold me - for you know how stern he was. And I never was allowed to go alone into the library. But I got interested in my book, and went on reading. So when he came in, I went on sitting there very still, with the book hidden under my skirt, for fear he should scold me. I thought perhaps before long papa'd go out for a second, to get some plates for his photography or something, and then I could slip away and never be noticed. The big window towards the garden was open, you remember, and I meant to jump out of it - as you did afterwards. It wasn't very high; and though the book was only The Vicar of Wakefield, he'd forbidden me to read it, and I was dreadfully afraid of him."

"Then you were there all the time?" Jack cried interrogatively. "And you heard our conversation - our whole conversation?"

"I was there all the time, Jack," I cried, in a fever of exaltation: "and I heard every word of it! It comes back to me now with a vividness like yesterday. I see the room before my eyes. I remember every syllable: I could repeat every sentence of it."

Jack drew a deep sigh of intense relief.

"Thank God for that!" he exclaimed, with profound gratitude. "Then I'm saved, and you're saved. We can both understand one another in that case. We know how it all happened!"

"Perfectly," I answered. "I know all now. As I sat there and cowered, I heard a knock at the door, and before papa could answer, you entered hastily. Papa looked round, I could hear, and saw who it was in a second.

"'Oh, it's you!' he said, coldly. 'It's you, Dr. Ivor. And pray, sir, what do you want here this evening?'"

"Go on!" Jack cried, intensely relieved, I could feel. "Let me see how much more you can remember, Una."

"So you shut the door softly and said:

"'Yes, it's I, Mr. Callingham,'" I continued all aglow, and looking into his eyes for confirmation. "'And I've come to tell you a fact that may surprise you. Prepare for strange news. Richard Wharton has returned to England!'

"I knew Richard Wharton was mamma's first husband, who was dead before I was born, as I'd always been told: and I sat there aghast at the news: it was so sudden, so crushing. I'd heard he'd been wrecked, and I thought he'd come to life again; but as yet I didn't suspect what was all the real meaning of it.

"But papa drew back, I could hear, in a perfect frenzy of rage, astonishment, and terror.

"'Richard Wharton!' he hissed out between his teeth, springing away like one stung. 'Richard Wharton come back! You liar! You sneak! He's dead this twenty years! You're trying to frighten me.'

"I never meant to overhear your conversation. But at that, it was so strange, I drew back and cowered even closer. I was afraid of papa's voice. I was afraid of his rage. He spoke just like a man who was ready to murder you.

"Then you began to talk with papa about strange things

that astonished me - strange things that I only half understood just then, but that by the light of what you've told me to-day I quite understand now - the history of my real father.

"'I'm no liar,' you answered. 'Richard Wharton has come back. And by the aid of what he's disclosed, I know the whole truth. The girl you call your daughter, and whose money you've stolen, is not yours at all. She's Richard Wharton's daughter Mary!'

"Papa staggered back a pace or two, and came quite close to the screen. I cowered behind it in alarm. I could see he was terrified. For a minute or two you talked with him, and urged him to confess. Bit by bit, as you went on, he recovered his nerve, and began to bluster. He didn't deny what you said: he saw it was no use: he just sneered and prevaricated.

"As I listened to his words, I saw he admitted it all. A great horror came over me. Then my life was one long lie! He was never my father. He had concocted a vile plot. He had held me in this slavery so many years to suit his own purposes. He had crushed my mother to death, and robbed me of my birthright. Even before that night, I never loved him. I thought it very wicked of me, but I never could love him. As he spoke to you and grew cynical, I began to loathe and despise him. I can't tell you how great a comfort it was to me to know - to hear from his own lips I was not that man's daughter.

"At last, after many recriminations, he looked across at you, and said, half laughing, for he was quite himself again by that time:

"'This is all very fine, Courtenay Ivor - all very fine in its way; but how are you going to prove it? that's the real question. Do you think any jury in England will believe, on your unsupported oath, such a cock-and-bull story? Do you think, even if Richard Wharton's come back, and you've got him on your side, I can't cross-examine all the life out of his body?'

"At that you said gravely - wanting to touch his conscience, I suppose: -

"'Richard Wharton's come back, but you can't cross-examine him. For Richard Wharton died some six or eight weeks since at my cottage at Babbicombe, after revealing to me all this vile plot against himself and his daughter.'

"Then papa drew back with a loud laugh - a hateful laugh like a demon's. I can't help calling him papa still, though it pains me even to think of him. That loud laugh rings still in my ears to this day. It was horrible, diabolical, like a wild beast's in triumph.

"'You fool!' he said, with a sneer. 'And you come here to tell me that! You infernal idiot! You come here to put yourself in my power like this! Courtenay Ivor, I always knew you were an ass, but I didn't ever know you were quite such a born idiot of a fellow as that. Hold back there, you image!' With a rapid dart, before you could see what he was doing, he passed a wire round your body and thrust two knobs into your hands. 'You're in my power now!' he exclaimed. 'You can't move or stir!'

"I saw at once what he'd done. He'd pinned you to the spot with the handles of his powerful electric apparatus. It was so strong that it would hold one riveted to the spot in pain. You couldn't let go. You could hardly even speak or cry aloud for help. He had pinned you down irresistibly. I thought he meant to murder you.

"Yet I was too terrified, even so, to scream aloud for the servants. I only crouched there, rooted, and wondered what next would happen.

"He went across to the door and turned the key in it. Then he opened the cabinet and took out some things there. It was growing quite dusk, and I could hardly see them. He returned with them where you stood, struggling in vain to set yourself free. His voice was as hard as adamant now. He spoke slowly and distinctly, in a voice like a fiend's. Oh, Jack, no wonder that scene took away my reason!"

"And you can remember what he said next, Una?" Jack asked, following me eagerly.

"Yes, I can remember what he said next," I went on. "He stood over you threateningly. I could see then the thing he held in his right hand was a loaded revolver. In his left was a bottle, a small medical phial.

"'If you stir, I'll shoot you,' he said; 'I'll shoot you like a dog! You fool, you've sealed your own fate! What an idiot to let me know Richard Wharton's dead! Now, hear your fate! Nobody saw you come into this house to-night. Nobody shall see you leave. Look here, sir, at this bottle. It's chloroform: do you understand? Chloroform - chloroform - chloroform! I shall hold it to your nose - so. I shall stifle you quietly - no blood, no fuss, no nasty mess of any sort. And when I'm done,

- do you see these flasks? – I can reduce your damned carcase to a pound of ashes with chemicals in half-an-hour! You've found out too much. But you've mistaken your man! Courtenay Ivor, say your prayers and commend your soul to the devil! You've driven me to bay, and I give you no quarter!'"

CHAPTER XXIII.

THE FATAL SHOT

"Thank God, Una," Jack cried, "you remember it now even better than I do!"

"Remember it!" I answered, holding my brow with my hands to keep the flood of thought from bursting it to fragments. "Remember it! Why, it comes back to me like waves of fire and burns me. I remember every word, every act, every gesture. I lifted my head slowly, Jack, and looked over the screen at him. In the twilight, I saw him there - the man I called my father - holding the bottle to your face, that wicked bottle of chloroform, with his revolver in one hand, and a calm smile like a fiend's playing hatefully and cruelly round that grave-looking mouth of his. I never saw any man look so ghastly in my life. I was rooted to the spot with awe and terror. I dared hardly cry out or move. Yet I knew this was murder. He would kill you! He would kill you! He was trying to poison you before my very eyes. Oh, heaven, how I hated him! He was no father of mine. He had never been my father. And he was murdering the man I loved best in the world. For I loved you better than life, Jack! Oh, the strain of it was terrible! I see it all now. I live it all over again. With one wild bound I leapt forward, and, hardly knowing what I did, I pressed the button, turned off the current from the battery, and rushed wildly upon him. I suppose the knob I pressed not only released you, but set the photographic machine at work automatically. But I didn't know it then. At any rate, I remember now, in the seconds that followed, flash came fast after flash. There was a sudden illumination. The room was lighter than day. It grew alternately bright as noon and then dark as pitch again by contrast. And by the light of the flashes, I saw you, half-dazed with the chloroform, standing helpless there.

"I rushed up and caught the man's arm. He was never my father! He dropped the bottle and struggled hard for possession of the pistol. First he pointed it at you, then at me, then at you again. He meant to shoot you. I was afraid it would go off. With a terrible effort I twisted his wrist awry, in the mad force of passion, and wrenched the revolver away from him. He jumped at my throat, still silent, but fierce like a tiger at bay. I eluded him, and sprang back. Then I remember no more, except that I stood with the pistol pointed at him. Next, came a flash, a loud roar. And then, in a moment, the Picture. He lay dead on the floor in his blood. And my Second State began. And from that day, for months, I was like a little child again."

Jack looked at me as I paused.

"And then?" he went on in a very low voice, half prompting me.

"And then all I can remember," I said, "is how you got out of the window. But I didn't know when I saw you, it was you or anyone else. That was my Second State then. The shot seemed to end all. What comes next is quite different. It belongs to the new world. There, my life stopped dead short and began all over again."

There was a moments silence. Jack was the first to break it.

"And now will you give yourself up to the police, Una?" he asked me quietly.

The question brought me back to the present again with a bound.

"Oh! what ought I to do?" I cried, wringing my hands. "I don't quite know all yet. Jack, why did you run away that last moment and leave me?"

Jack took my hand very seriously.

"Una, my child," he said, fixing his eyes on mine, "I hardly know whether I can ever make you understand all that. I must ask you at first at least just simply to believe me. I must ask you to trust me and to accept my account. When you rushed upon me as I stood there, all entangled in that hateful apparatus, and unable to move, I didn't know where you had been; I didn't know how you'd come there. But I felt sure you must have heard at least your false father's last words - that he'd stifle me with the chloroform and burn my body up afterwards to ashes with his chemicals. You seized the pistol before I could quite recover from the effects of the fumes. He lay dead at my feet before I realised what was happening.

"Then, in a moment, as I looked at you, I took it all in, like a flash of lightning. I saw how impossible it would be ever to convince anybody else of the truth of our story. I saw if we both told the truth, no one would ever believe us. There was no time then to reflect, no time to hesitate. I had to make up my mind at once to a plan of action, and to carry it out without a second's delay. In one burst of inspiration, I saw that to stop would be to seal both our fates. I didn't mind so much for myself; that was nothing, nothing: but for your sake I felt I must dare and risk everything. Then I turned round and looked at you. I saw at one glance the horror of the moment had rendered you speechless and almost senseless. The right plan came to me at once as if by magic. 'Una,' I cried, 'stand back! Wait till the servants come!' For I knew the report of the revolver would soon bring them up to the library. Then I waited myself. As they reached the door, and forced it open, I jumped up to the window. Just outside, my bicycle stood propped against the wall. I let them purposely catch just a glimpse of my back - an unfamiliar figure. They saw the pistol on the floor, - Mr. Callingham dead - you, startled and horrified - a man unknown, escaping in hot haste from the window. I risked my own life, so as to save your name and honour. I let them see me escape, so as to exonerate you from suspicion. If they hanged me, what matter? Then I leapt down in a hurry, jumped lightly on my machine, and rode off like the wind down the avenue to the high-road. For a second or two they waited to look at you and your father. That second or two saved us. By the time they'd come out to look, I was away down the grounds, past the turn of the avenue, and well on for the high-road. They'd seen a glimpse of the murderer, escaping by the window. They would never suspect YOU. You were saved, and I was happy."

"And for the same reason even now," I said, "you wouldn't tell the police?"

"Let sleeping dogs lie," Jack answered, in the same words as Dr. Marten. "Why rake up this whole matter? It's finished for ever now, and nobody but yourself is ever likely to reopen it. If we both told our tale, we might run a great risk of being seriously misinterpreted. You know it's true; so do I: but who else would believe us? No man's bound to criminate himself. You shot him to save my life, at the very moment when you first learned all his cruelty and his vileness. The rest of the world could never be made to understand all that. They'd say to the end, as it looks on the surface, 'She shot her father to save her lover.'"

"You're right," I said slowly. "I shall let this thing rest. But the photographs, Jack - the apparatus - the affair of the inquest?"

"That was all very simple," Jack answered. "For a day or two, of course, I was in a frantic state of mind for fear you should be suspected, or the revolver should betray you. But though I saw the electric sparks, of course, I knew nothing about the photographs. I wasn't even aware that the apparatus took negatives automatically. And I was so full of the terrible reports in the newspapers about your sudden loss of health, that I could think of nothing else - least of all my own safety. As good luck would have it, however, the clergyman at Wrode, who knew the Wilsons, happened to speak to me of the murder - all England called it the murder and talked of nothing else for at least a fortnight, - and in the course of conversation he mentioned this apparatus of Mr. Callingham's construction. 'What a pity,' he said, 'there didn't happen to be one of them in the library at the time! If it was focussed towards the persons, and had been set on by the victim, it would have photographed the whole scene the murder, the murderer.'

"That hint revealed much to me. As he spoke, I remembered suddenly about those mysterious flashes when you burst all at once on my sight from behind the screen. Till that moment, I thought of them only as some result of your too suddenly turning off the electric current. But then, it came home to me in a second that Mr. Callingham must have set out his apparatus all ready for experimenting - that the electric apparatus was there to put it in working order. The button you turned must not only have stopped the current that nailed me writhing to the spot: it must also have set working the automatic photographic camera!

"That thought, as you may imagine, filled me with speechless alarm: for I remembered then that one of the flashes broke upon us at the exact moment when you fired the pistol. Such a possibility was horrible to contemplate. The photographs by themselves could give no clue to our conversation or to the events that compelled you, almost against your own will, to fire that fatal shot. If they were found by the police, all would be up with both of us. They might hang ME if they liked: except for Elsie's sake, I didn't mind much about that: but for your safety, come what might, I felt I must manage to get hold of them or to destroy them.

"Were the negatives already in the hands of the police? That was now the great question. I read the reports diligently, with all their descriptions of the room, and noticed that while the table, the alcove, the screen, the box, the electrical apparatus, were all carefully mentioned, not a word was said anywhere about the possession of the negatives. Reasoning further upon the description of the supposed murderer as given by

Grant Allen

the servants, and placarded broadcast in every town in England, I came to the conclusion that the police couldn't yet have discovered the existence of these negatives: for some of them must surely have photographed my face, however little in focus; while the printed descriptions mentioned only the man's back, as the servants saw him escaping from the window. The papers said the room was being kept closed till the inquest, for inspection in due time by the coroner's jury. I made up my mind at once. When the room was opened for the jurors to view it, I must get in there and carry them off, if they caught me in the attempt.

"It was no use trying before the jury had seen the room. But as soon as that was all over, I judged the strictness of the watch upon the premises would be relaxed, and the windows would probably be opened a little to air the place. So on the morning of the inquest, I told the Wilsons casually I'd met you at Torquay and had therefore a sort of interest in learning the result of the coroner's deliberation. Then I took my bicycle, and rode across to Woodbury. Leaning up my machine against the garden wall, I walked carelessly in at the gate, and up the walk to the library window, as if the place belonged to me. Oh, how my heart beat as I looked in and wondered! The folding halves were open, and the box stood on the table, still connected with the wires that conducted the electrical current. I stood and hesitated in alarm. Were the negatives still there, or had the police discovered them? If they were gone, all was up with you. The game was lost. No jury on earth, I felt sure, would believe my story.

"I vaulted up to the sill. Thank heaven, I was athletic. Not a soul was about: but I heard a noise of muffled voices in the other rooms behind. Treading cat-like across the floor, I turned the key in the lock. A chalk mark still showed the position of the pistol on the ground exactly as you flung it. The box was on the table, and I saw at a glance, the wires which connected it with the battery had never been disconnected. I was afraid of receiving a shock if I touched them with my hands, and I had no time to waste in discovering electrical attachments. So I pulled out my knife, and you can fancy with what trembling hands I cut that wire on either side and released the box from its dangerous connections. I knew only too well the force of that current. Then I took the thing under my arm, leaped from the window once more, and ran across the shrubbery towards the spot where I'd left my bicycle.

"On the way, the thought struck me that if I carried along the camera, all would be up with me should I happen to be challenged. It was the only one of the sort in existence at the time, and the wires at the side would at once suffice to identify it and to arouse the suspicion even of an English policeman. I paused for a moment behind a thick clump of lilacs and tried to pull out the incriminating negatives. Oh, Una, I did it for your sake; but there, terrified and trembling, in hiding behind the bushes, and in danger of my life, with that still more unspeakable danger for yours haunting me always like a nightmare, can you wonder that for the moment I almost felt myself a murderer? The very breezes in the trees made my heart give a jump, and then stand still within me. I got out the first two or three plates with some trifling difficulty, for I didn't understand the automatic apparatus then as I understand it now: but the fourth stuck hard for a minute; the fifth broke in two; and the sixth - well, the sixth plate baffled me entirely by getting jammed in the clockwork, and refusing to move, either backward or forward.

"At that moment, I either heard or fancied I heard a loud noise of pursuit, a hue and cry behind me. Zeal for your safety had made me preternaturally nervous. I looked about me hurriedly, thrust the negatives I'd recovered into my breast-pocket as fast as ever I could, flung the apparatus away from me with the sixth plate jammed hard in the groove, and made off at the top of my speed for the wall behind me. For there, at that critical point, it occurred to me suddenly that the sixth and last flash of the machine had come and gone just as I stood poising myself on the ledge of the window-sill; and I thought to myself - rightly as it turned out - this additional evidence would only strengthen the belief in the public mind that Mr. Callingham had been murdered by the man whom the servants saw escaping from the window.

"The rest, my child, you know pretty well already. In a panic on your account, I scrambled over the wall, tearing my hands as I went with that nasty-bottle glass, reached my bicycle outside, and made off, not for the country, but for the inn where they were holding the coroner's inquest. My left hand I had to hold, tied up in my handkerchief to stop the bleeding, in the pocket of my jacket: but I thought this the best way, all the same, to escape detection. And, indeed, instead of being, as I feared, the only man there in bicycling dress and knickerbockers, I found the occasion had positively attracted all the cyclists of the neighbourhood. Each man went there to show his own innocence of fear or suspicion. A good dozen or two of bicyclists stood gathered already in the body of the room in the same incriminating costume. So I found safety in numbers. Even the servants who had seen me disappear through the window, though their eyes lighted upon me more than once, never for a moment seemed to suspect me. And I know very well why. When I stand up, I'm the straightest and most perpendicular man that ever walked erect. But when I poise to jump, I bend my spine so much that I produce the impression of being almost hump-backed. It was that attitude you recognised in me when I jumped from the window just now."

"Why, Jack," I cried clinging to him in a perfect whirlwind of wonder, "one can hardly believe it - that was only an hour ago!"

"That was only an hour ago," Jack answered, smiling. "But as for you, I suppose you've lived half a lifetime again in it. And now you know the whole secret of the Woodbury Mystery. And you won't want to give yourself up to the police any longer."

CHAPTER XXIV.

ALL'S WELL THAT ENDS WELL

But why didn't you explain it all to me at the very first?" I exclaimed, all tremulous. "When you met me at Quebec, I mean - why didn't you tell me then? Did you and Elsie come there on purpose to meet me?"

"Yes, we came there to meet you," Jack answered. "But we were afraid to make ourselves known to you all at once just at first, because, you see, Una, I more than half suspected then, what I know now to be the truth, that you were coming out to Canada on purpose to hunt me up, not as your friend and future husband, but in enmity and suspicion as your father's murderer. And in any case we were uncertain which attitude you might adopt towards me. But I see I must explain a little more even now. I haven't told you yet why I came at all to Canada."

"Tell me now," I answered. "I must know everything to-day. I can never rest now till I've heard the whole story."

"Well," Jack went on more calmly, "after the first excitement wore off in the public mind, there came after a bit a lull of languid interest; the papers began to forget the supposed facts of the murder, and to dwell far more upon your own new role as a pyschological curiosity. They talked much about your strange new life and its analogies elsewhere. I was anxious to see you, of course, to satisfy myself of your condition; but the doctors who had charge of you refused to let you mix for a while with anyone you had known in your First State; and I now think wisely. It was best you should recover your general health and faculties by slow degrees, without being puzzled and distracted by constant upsetting recollections and suggestions of your past history.

"But for me, of course, at the time, the separation was terrible. Each morning, I read with feverish interest the reports of your health, and longed, day after day, to hear of some distinct improvement. And yet at the same time, I was terrified at every approach to complete convalescence: I feared that if you got better at all, you might remember too quick, and that then the sudden rush of recollection might kill you or upset your reason. But by-and-by, it became clear to me you could remember nothing of the actual shot itself. And I saw plainly why. It was the firing of the pistol that obliterated, as it were, every trace of your past life in your disorganised brain. And it obliterated ITSELF too. Your new life began just one moment later, with the Picture of the dead man stretched before you in his blood on the floor, and a figure in the background disappearing through the window."

How clever he was, to be sure! I saw in a moment Jack had interpreted my whole frame of mind correctly and wonderfully.

"Well, I went back to Babbicombe," Jack continued, "and, lest my heart should break for want of human sympathy, I confided every word of my terrible story to Elsie. Elsie can trust me; and Elsie believed me. Gradually, as you began to recover, I realised the soundness of your doctor's idea that you should be allowed to come back to yourself by re-education from the very beginning, without any too early intrusion of reminiscences from your previous life to confuse and disturb you. But I couldn't go on with my profession, all the same, while I waited. I couldn't attend as I ought to my patients' wants and ailments: I was too concentrated upon you: the strain was too great upon me. So I threw up my practice, came out to Canada, bought a bit of land, and began farming here, and seeing a few patients now and again locally, just to fill up my time with. I felt confident in the end you would recover and remember me. I felt confident you would come to yourself and marry me. But still, it was very long work waiting. Every month, Elsie got news indirectly from Minnie Moore or someone of your state of health; and I intended to go back and try to see you as soon as ever you were in a condition to bear the shock of re-living your previous life again.

"Unfortunately, however, the police got hold of YOU before I could carry my plan into execution. As soon as I heard that, I made up my mind at once to go home by the first mail and break it all gently to you. So Elsie and I started for Quebec, meaning to sail by the Dominion steamer for England. But at the hotel at Quebec we saw the telegrams announcing that you were then on your way out to Canada. Well, of course we didn't feel sure whether you came as a friend or an enemy. We were certain it was to seek me out you were coming to America; but whether you remembered me still and still loved me, or whether you'd found out some stray clue to the missing man, and were anxious to hunt me down as your father's murderer, we hadn't the slightest conception. So under those circumstances, we thought it best not to meet you ourselves at the steamer, or to reveal our identity too soon, for fear of a catastrophe. I knew it would be better to wait and watch - to gain your confidence, if possible - in any case, to find out how you were affected on first seeing us and talking with us.

"Well then, as the time came on for the Sarmatian to arrive, it began to strike me by degrees that all Quebec was agog with curiosity to see you. I dared not go down to meet you at the quay myself; but the Chief Constable of Quebec, Major Tascherel, was an old friend and fellow-officer of my father's; and when I explained to him my fears that you might be mobbed by sightseers on your arrival at the harbour, and told him how afraid I was of the shock it might give you to meet an old friend unexpectedly at the steamer's side, he very kindly consented to go down and see you safe through the Custom House, It was so lucky I knew him. If it hadn't been for that, you might have been horribly inconvenienced.

"As you may imagine, when we first saw you get into the Pullman car, both Elsie and I felt our hearts come up into our months with suspense and anxiety. We'd arranged it all so on purpose, for we felt sure you were on your way to Palmyra to find us: but when it came to the actual crisis, we wondered most nervously what effect the sight of us might have upon your system. But in a moment, I saw you didn't remember us at all, or only vaguely attached to us some faint sense of friendliness. That was well, because it enabled us to gain your confidence easily. As we spoke with you, the sense of friendly interest deepened. I knew that, all unconsciously to yourself, you loved me still, and that in a very short time, if only I could see you and be with you, I might bring all back to you."

Jack paused and looked at me. As he paused, I felt my old self revive again more completely than ever with a rush.

"Oh, Jack," I cried, "so you HAVE done; so you HAVE brought all back to me! My Second State's over: I'm the same girl you used to know at Torquay once more. I remember everything - everything - such a world - such a lifetime! I feel as if my head would burst with all the things I remember. I don't know what to do with it. I'm so tired, so weary."

"Lay it here," Jack said simply.

And I laid it on his shoulder, just as I used to do years ago, and cried so long in silence, and was ever so much comforted. For I've admitted all along that I'm only a woman.

There we sat, hand in hand, for many minutes more, saying never another word, but sympathising silently, till Elsie returned from Palmyra.

When she burst into the room, she called out lightly as she entered:

"Well, I've got you your lemon, Una, and I do hope -" Then she broke short suddenly. "Oh, Jack," she cried, faltering, and half guessing the truth, "what's the meaning of this? Why, Una's been crying. You bad boy, you've been frightening her. I oughtn't to have left her ten minutes alone with you!"

Jack rose and held up his hand in warning.

"Don't talk to her at present, Elsie," he said. "You needn't be afraid. Una's found out everything. She remembers all now. And she knows how everything happened. And she's borne it so bravely, without any more shock to her health and strength than was absolutely inevitable. - Let her sleep if she can. It'll do her so much good. - But, Elsie, there's one thing I want to say to you both before I hand her over to you. After all that's happened, I don't think Una'll want to hear that hateful name of Callingham any more. It never was really hers, and it never shall be. We'll let bygones be bygones in every other respect, and not rake up any details of that hateful story. But she's been Una to us always, and she shall be Una still. It's a very good name for her: for there's only one of her. But next week, I propose, she shall be Una Ivor."

I threw myself on his neck, and cried again like a child.

"I accept, Jack," I said, sobbing. "Let it be Ivor, if you will. Next week, then, I'll be your wife at last, my darling!"

www.ingramcontent.com/pod-product-compliance
Lightning Source LLC
Chambersburg PA
CBHW030316180626
46810CB00003B/1101